It Came from the Deep

A. G. Cascone

Troll

For Richard A. Fazzari
for working so hard
to pull us out of the shark tank

CHAPTER 1

Randi Carson didn't dare move a muscle. She just stared straight ahead at the killer that was steadily approaching.

Randi could feel her heart pounding against her chest as the massive shark cut through the water like a torpedo. Its bloodthirsty eyes held her in a deadly stare.

Just a few feet away from her now, the shark began to open its mouth. Randi could see the rows of jagged, razor-sharp teeth and the grisly remains of its last meal.

Randi had read books about sharks. They said that a shark's teeth were so sharp, and its jaws so powerful, its victims didn't even feel the pain when the shark chomped down on them. Still . . .

Just then the shark opened its jaws wide—wide enough to swallow her whole!

Randi let out a scream and jumped backward.

"Look out!" a voice warned her suddenly.

Randi turned to see a boy who was about her age wincing in pain. "You stepped on my foot," he said.

"Sorry," she apologized, feeling embarrassed about the way she'd freaked out.

"No problem," he answered, shrugging it off. "The sharks can't hurt you, you know," he went on. "They're behind Plexiglas."

"I know," Randi answered, feeling even more embarrassed now.

Then the boy smiled. "This is a pretty cool place, don't you think?"

Randi nodded. "Really cool," she said, looking around.

The two of them were standing inside a Plexiglas tunnel that ran along the bottom of the shark lagoon. Sharks swam all around them, even over their heads. It was as if they were underwater *with* all the sharks.

"My name's Garrett Brown." The boy introduced himself.

"I'm Randi Carson."

"Nice to meet you, Randi." Garrett smiled. "So how long are you going to be here on the island?"

"Three more days," Randi answered. She and her family had been there for one day already. "My parents won this vacation from a cola cap."

"You're kidding!" Garrett exclaimed. "Mine too! Actually, it was *my* bottle of soda that had the winning cap."

Randi smiled. "I've never been to a Caribbean island before," she told Garrett. "It's so beautiful here. The sand is so white and the water is so blue, just like in the pictures. And it's *soooo* warm, which is really cool. Back home, there's more than a foot of snow on the ground."

"Yeah," Garrett agreed. "This place is pretty terrific. I guess that's why they call it 'Paradise.'"

"I think the best part about this resort is these underwater tunnels," Randi said.

"Me too," Garrett said. "Have you been down here at night?"

Randi shook her head.

"Now that's *really* cool. And *really* creepy," he told her. "When the sun's not shining, it's much harder to look up and see the surface of the water. You really feel like you're standing at the bottom of the sea."

"The fish are so close," Randi added. "It's almost as though you could reach out and touch them." Randi did reach out to touch the Plexiglas as a school of bright yellow fish swam slowly by. "Isn't it amazing how the fish don't seem to be bothered by us? They act as if we're not even here."

"Except for the sharks," Garrett pointed out.

Another shark was headed their way with its mouth wide open. It was looking at Randi and Garrett as if they were shark chow. Randi shuddered. "I hate sharks," she said, stepping away from the glass.

"Oh, really?" Garrett chuckled. "Then what are you doing down here in the first place?"

The truth was that Randi *was* there to look at the sharks. Even though they terrified her, she was fascinated by them as well. She didn't know why. And she certainly couldn't begin to explain it to Garrett. "I came to see the other fish," she told him.

It wasn't a lie. She really did like to watch the colorful fish.

"Being down here is almost as cool as scuba diving," Garrett said.

"You've been scuba diving?" Randi asked. That was something she wanted to do during this vacation.

"Yeah," Garrett answered. "I went with my dad yesterday. It was really fun. Today, I thought I'd go out on one of those Sea-Doos."

"Are they those things that look like water motor-cycles?" Randi asked.

Garrett nodded. "They're way better than the Jet Skis," he told her. "They're much bigger, and the seats are really cool. Want to come with me?"

"Sure." Randi was thrilled to have someone her own age to hang out with. "That'll be fun."

"Great," Garrett said. "Let's go."

As Randi and Garrett made their way through the tunnel, Randi watched the fish swim around them. There were fish of every size and every color. Most of them stayed in schools, swimming through beds of seaweed or coral, over and under rocks. Some even tried to bury themselves in the gravelly floor.

"Look at that!" Randi pointed up as a giant sea turtle glided by overhead.

They stopped walking and watched the turtle make its way to the surface.

"What's that?" Garrett asked.

Randi followed his gaze. He was looking at a rock above the surface of the water. There was something on the rock that seemed to be moving. "It looks like a person," Randi said, struggling to make out the blurry image. She thought it was a man wearing a bright red fishing cap and black rubber boots.

"What's that guy doing out in the middle of the shark lagoon?" Garrett asked.

Sharks of every size, breed, and color began to gather, circling the rock. The hammerheads pounded their way past the nurse sharks, while the tiger sharks and the makos closed in. They all seemed to be focused on the man on the rock.

"He'd better be careful," Randi said nervously.

Before she'd even gotten out the last word, there was a huge *splash*.

Suddenly, the sharks went into a frenzy, whipping around wildly. The water started churning and bubbling.

Randi couldn't see the surface anymore. "What's going on?"

"Where's the guy who was on the rock?" Garrett said in a panic.

"You don't think . . ." Randi's words trailed off.

Her question was answered by a sudden explosion of color in the water. It was red . . . blood red.

CHAPTER 2

"The man fell off the rock!" Randi shrieked. "He's in the water with the sharks!"

The red cloud in the water spread wider and wider as the bloodthirsty sharks attacked from every side.

"We'd better go get help!" Garrett cried. He took off running.

Randi followed him through the tunnel toward the exit, moving as fast as she could. But there was no way they'd be able to get help in time.

Randi finally saw the light at the end of the tunnel. She panted as she followed Garrett up the incline.

"Help!" Garrett shouted, racing for the walkway above the water. "There's a man being eaten by sharks!"

"Help!" Randi screamed, following Garrett onto the path. "Someone, please help!"

But there was no one around. The two of them were all alone.

Suddenly, they heard a chuckle behind them. Randi turned toward the sound.

"What are you two kids hollering about?" a man with a bright red fishing cap and black rubber boots asked. It was the same man they'd seen from inside the tunnel.

Randi pressed both hands against her chest as if she were trying to keep her heart from exploding. "We thought you had fallen into the water with the sharks," she told the man. "We were scared to death!"

The man just laughed.

"It's not funny," Garrett yelled. "Look," he added, pointing to the pool of red blood swirling in the blue water. "There's blood in that water. Maybe those sharks attacked someone else!"

"The sharks haven't attacked anything but their food," the man told them. "I'm feeding them."

"What are you feeding them?" Randi shrieked. "People?"

"I'm feeding them chum," the man answered. "See?" He lifted one of the buckets at his feet and tipped it toward them so that they could see the bloody chum inside. "It's fish guts," he explained.

"Oh, gross." Garrett turned away.

Randi covered her eyes.

"It's not gross," the man said, dumping the contents of the bucket into the water. "It's what they eat."

"It's still gross," Randi insisted.

"It's actually kind of tasty," the man said. He reached into the next bucket and scooped some out in his hand. "Want to try a bite?"

Randi looked at the red-stained glop that dripped through the man's fingers. "You've got to be kidding," she said.

But the man didn't show even the hint of a smile. Randi had the feeling that he wasn't kidding at all.

"How about you?" he asked Garrett, waving the guts in his face.

"No way!" Garrett told him, moving away.

The man shrugged. "Your loss." Then he dropped the chum into the lagoon.

Three sharks shot to the surface to get at the small clump of guts.

Randi and Garrett jumped back.

"They're really dangerous, aren't they?" Randi asked the shark feeder.

"Not to me," the man said. "Now, barracudas are another story. They're testy little buggers. You don't ever want to get on the bad side of a barracuda. See this scar on my face?"

Randi and Garrett both nodded. They couldn't help but notice it. The scar ran from his eyebrow to his chin in an ugly, jagged line.

"I got this from a barracuda," he told them. "A real slimy little creep."

"But you think sharks are okay?" Randi asked, confused.

The man just smiled, showing his pointed, yellow-stained teeth. This guy was totally weird.

"Sharks are much more dangerous than barracudas,"

Garrett said. "I've even heard people around this resort talking about several shark attacks on people staying on other islands."

Randi had heard the same rumors.

But before she had the chance to say so, a loud alarm went off. It sounded like a fire drill. But it wasn't.

"Time for the two of you to get to rehearsal for the Feast of Nanuwee," the shark feeder snapped. "You'd better hurry too. You'll be in big trouble if you're late."

Randi sighed. She'd forgotten all about the Feast of Nanuwee rehearsals. It looked like the Sea-Doos were out.

"Get going," the shark feeder ordered.

Neither Randi nor Garrett bothered to argue with him. They just walked away, up the path toward the main building of the hotel.

"The Feast of Nanuwee," Garrett griped once they were out of earshot. "Is that the dumbest thing you've ever heard of, or what?"

"For real," Randi agreed. "But my parents said I'm not allowed to complain about it. After all, we are getting a free vacation. So if the people who run this resort want us to join in some stupid celebration for somebody named Nanuwee, we'd better do it."

"I guess," Garrett said.

The Feast of Nanuwee was the reason the resort was giving away the free trips in the first place. It was some kind of promotional stunt. Everybody on the island had a part to play.

"I'm in stick-clapping class," Randi told Garrett. That

was her part in the feast, clapping sticks together in time with the drums.

"Me too," Garrett told her. "I didn't see you at practice yesterday."

"I was there," Randi groaned. "I guess we just didn't notice one another. There are a lot of kids in the stick-clapping group."

"That's true." Suddenly a grin spread across Garrett's face. "I'll bet they wouldn't notice if two of us were missing."

"What are you saying?" Randi smiled. She knew exactly what Garrett saying—and she liked it.

"Let's skip it."

"And do what?" Randi asked.

"Go out on Sea-Doos," Garrett answered. "It'll be perfect because everybody else will be at rehearsal for the Feast of Nanuwee."

"I don't know," Randi said. "My parents might get mad if I skip the rehearsal."

"They won't even notice," Garrett assured her. "The adult groups aren't near the stick-clapping pavilion."

Garrett had a point. Her parents wouldn't even know that she'd skipped her rehearsal. So as Garrett turned off the path and headed for the beach, Randi followed.

The beach was deserted. Randi and Garrett had it all to themselves.

This is really going to be fun, Randi thought.

They headed for the shack where the Sea-Doos were stored, approaching it from behind. As they got closer to the shack, they heard voices coming from inside.

Garrett put a finger to his lips to tell Randi to stay quiet. They slowed their pace, silently moving up to the back wall of the shack. Then they listened.

"I can't wait until this feast is finished," someone said. It was a woman's voice.

"Soon," a man's voice answered.

"Not soon enough for me," the woman groaned. "I can't believe we have to go to the other islands to feed. There's plenty to eat right here."

"I know," the man replied. "But we don't want anybody to get suspicious."

A beeping sound interrupted their conversation. It sounded like the beeper that Randi's dad had on his watch to remind him to do one thing or another.

"I've got to go," the woman said. "I have to teach a class for the Feast of Nanuwee."

"And I've got to get into the water," the man said. "My twelve hours are up."

Randi and Garrett plastered themselves against the back wall of the shack, hoping they wouldn't get caught. They watched in silence as the woman strode off along the beach toward the path.

But what about the man? Where is he? Randi wondered.

It was Garrett who got up the courage to move first. Randi tried to stop him, but he shook her off. He crept slowly along the back of the shack, then peeked around the corner. He looked back at Randi and shrugged. Then he inched his way around the shack, sticking close to the side of it.

Randi began to follow. By the time she reached the corner, Garrett was in front of the shack.

"He's gone," Garrett told her.

Randi stepped out into the open. "Where did he go?" she asked.

"I don't know." Garrett said. "And I don't care. Finally, we can grab a Sea-Doo and have some fun." He headed into the shack to do just that.

But Randi was still nervous. She knew that the woman had walked in the direction of the hotel, but she wanted to make sure that the man wouldn't come back and catch them doing something they weren't supposed to be doing.

There were footprints in the sand that led toward the water.

Randi looked toward the sea, but no one was out there.

Where the heck did he go? Randi wondered. Slowly, she started to follow the footprints. She followed them all the way to the water's edge.

That was when she discovered that there was something terribly wrong.

CHAPTER

3

Randi stood staring down at the strange footprints in the wet sand. *How can this be?* she thought, blinking hard at the sight.

Behind her, in the dry sand, the footprints looked normal. They had heels and arches and five separate toes. But the footprints in front of her weren't human. In fact, they looked like the footprints of a giant duck, flat and webbed.

"Garrett," Randi called up the beach. "Look at this."

"What?" Garrett asked, without looking her way. He was much more interested in picking out a Sea-Doo.

"That guy's footprints," Randi answered. "They lead out to the sea."

"So?" Garrett questioned, still paying no attention. "Maybe he swam over to the other island."

Randi rolled her eyes. "Yeah, well, he's not in the water," she shot back. "And his footprints look like a duck's. At least the footprints that are down here."

"So what?" Garrett asked. "One of the kids in my neighborhood has duck feet too. He's got like six webbed toes on one foot. It's no big deal."

"These aren't just regular webbed toes," Randi told him. "They're really weird. Come look," she insisted.

"Oh, brother," Garrett huffed as he headed down the beach toward Randi. "I don't want to look at weird toes. I want to ride the Sea-Doos."

"Look at the footprints up there," Randi told him as he approached. "Then take a look at these."

But as Garrett reached the wet sand, a crystal-blue wave rolled to the shore, erasing all footprints in sight.

"You missed them!" Randi moaned.

Garrett shrugged. Then he changed the subject back to the one he was interested in, the Sea-Doos.

"There's only one Sea-Doo up there we can ride," he told Randi. "The rest of them are chained up. Do you want to take turns riding it, or do you want to ride it together?"

"I don't know." Randi shrugged. "Have you ever ridden a Sea-Doo before?"

"Lots of times," Garrett answered. "Haven't you?"

Randi shook her head no.

"Then why don't we ride together," Garrett suggested. "I'll drive first so that I can show you how to steer."

"Are you sure we won't get into trouble?" Randi asked.

"For what?" Garrett said. "The Sea-Doos are free. The

guests are allowed to ride them anytime they want. Only now we won't have to wait in line."

"Then how come they're chained up?" she asked.

"Because the beach guys probably knew that if they didn't chain them up, nobody would go to those stupid Nanuwee classes today," he answered.

Randi was sure Garrett was right. Who wanted to be in stick-clapping class when they could be out in the water Sea-Dooing? Besides, even her parents had said it was okay for her to ride the Sea-Doos. So what difference did it make *when* she decided to ride them?

"Let's do it!" Randi cried, racing for the Sea-Doo. She threw her leg over the backseat as if she were climbing onto a motorcycle.

Garrett started to laugh. "We have to push it down to the water first," he told her. "And you have to wear one of these." He reached for a stack of safety vests piled up by the shack and held one out to Randi.

"Oh," Randi said, feeling embarrassed. She climbed off and put on the safety vest.

Garrett pushed the blue Sea-Doo down to the water. "Now you can get on," he said as it hit the sea and bobbed up and down with the current.

The two of them climbed aboard. "You ready?" Garrett asked over his shoulder.

"Ready as I'll ever be," Randi replied, feeling excited and scared at the same time.

Garrett turned the key to start the engine. "Driving a Sea-Doo is easy. See?"

Randi peered over Garrett's shoulder as he twisted the handle just a bit.

The engine gurgled and the Sea-Doo lurched forward.

"Too cool," Randi told him as they began to float slowly away from the shore.

"The more you twist," Garrett said, "the faster you'll go."

Randi grabbed Garrett's waist as he started to demonstrate. Within seconds, they were sailing across the top of the water.

"This is great!" Randi exclaimed as the wind whipped through her curly brown hair. She could feel the hot sun beating down on her face as the cool sea water sprayed up around her.

"You okay?" Garrett screamed back over the roar of the engine as they bounced over a wave.

"You bet!" Randi shouted.

"Now all you have to do to stop moving is stop twisting the handle," he said, demonstrating again.

The Sea-Doo quickly glided to a halt.

"See how easy it is?" Garrett asked, turning around.

"Seems like a piece of cake," Randi answered.

"The only thing you have to remember is not to go past those buoys out there." Garrett pointed to the red and blue floats several hundred feet in front of them. "The water gets too deep," he explained. "You want me to head back to shore so we can switch places and you can try driving?"

"Okay," Randi agreed. She clung on to Garrett as they sped back to the beach.

"Just twist the handle slowly," Garrett instructed, as

Randi took the driver's seat. "If you get nervous, let go and we'll come to a stop. Okay?"

"Got it," Randi said. She twisted the handle and headed cautiously back out to sea. Being on the back of the Sea-Doo was fun, but driving it was a blast!

Within a few minutes, Randi was sailing at full speed.

"You're doing great!" Garrett shouted, hanging on to her waist.

Randi *was* doing great. She was even starting to hit the waves head on so that the Sea-Doo would fly a foot or so into the air. She was beginning to feel like a real dare-devil—until she saw the red and blue buoys bouncing in the water just a few feet ahead.

"Slow down," Garrett told her. "We have to turn. But don't turn too fast or we might—"

Randi never heard the end of Garrett's sentence. She was so panicked by the thought of ending up in deep waters that she turned to the left so hard and so fast, the Sea-Doo rolled over right on top of them.

Salt water filled Randi's mouth and nose as she struggled to get out from under the Sea-Doo.

Luckily, Garrett managed to push it away, and the two of them surfaced at the same time.

"We've got big problems," Garrett said, coughing. "We're never going to be able to get this thing upright. It's too heavy."

But Randi barely heard him. She was paying attention to another problem—a much bigger problem than a tipped-over Sea-Doo.

Less than twenty feet past the red and blue buoys, a big, black, triangular fin cut through the surface of the water. It was heading swiftly toward them.

"Garrett!" Randi cried. "There's a shark out here!"

"What?" Garrett yelped, struggling to tread water.

"A shark!" Randi repeated, pointing toward the fin. "Swim for the shore!" she screamed, paddling frantically.

Garrett started swimming too, moving even more quickly than Randi.

Randi kept her eyes on the shoreline as she stroked as fast and furiously as she could. She was afraid to look back to see if the shark was gaining on them.

Please don't let him get us! Randi thought.

Suddenly, she felt her right foot kick more than the water. She was sure it was the shark, sure that at any moment she would be bitten right in two.

Something closed down around Randi's left ankle— hard. So hard that Randi didn't even feel pain as she was pulled under the water.

CHAPTER 4

Help me! Randi tried to scream as another tug on her ankle pulled her deeper underwater.

Randi kicked out with her free foot. Just then the shark yanked backward, and Randi hit the sea bottom hard. She was sure the shark was going to chomp through her bone and bite off her foot.

Let go of me! Randi pleaded soundlessly, thrashing about in terror. She could feel the grains of sand and broken shells scraping her skin as the shark continued dragging her out to sea.

He wasn't going to bite off her foot! He was going to swallow her whole!

Noooooooo! Randi kicked out again. This time she hit the shark's snout. Suddenly, both legs were free and Randi was propelling herself forward, back toward the shore.

23

Finally, she managed to scramble to her feet and run for the beach. She could see Garrett racing up the sand ahead of her. Randi wasn't even sure that he realized what had happened to her. She was just about to scream for him when another shout stopped her.

"Hold it right there," a voice behind Randi boomed.

Randi spun around fast, half-expecting to see the shark chasing her onto the beach. But it wasn't a shark. It was the man they had heard in the Sea-Doo shack. Randi recognized his voice. But now he wasn't walking *into* the sea, he was walking out of it, dragging the Sea-Doo along with him.

Behind him, in the clear blue water, there wasn't a shark fin in sight.

"What do you think you're doing?" the man barked.

Randi couldn't believe her eyes. Maybe it wasn't a shark that had grabbed her. Maybe it was the hotel worker. But how was that possible? Randi was sure that she hadn't seen a man in the water. And sure that she *had* seen a fin.

"You're supposed to be rehearsing for the Feast of Nanuwee!" the hotel worker continued to growl. "Didn't you see the rules in your vacation pamphlet? The only reason you're getting a free vacation here is because you and your families have agreed to participate in the Feast of Nanuwee! If you don't participate, you're out of here!"

Randi swallowed hard. Facing this guy was almost more frightening than facing a shark.

"We were just headed over to our stick-clapping class,"

Garrett lied as he hurried back to where Randi stood.

"On a Sea-Doo?" the man snarled.

Now Garrett swallowed hard.

"Let me tell you something, kid," the man said as he dragged the Sea-Doo onto dry sand. "Mr. C. is going to bite both your heads off for this."

"Mr. C.?" Randi squeaked out the name. "Who's that?"

"The owner of this resort," the guy answered. "The great Carcharodon Carcharias," he said, bowing his head. "Founder of Paradise."

"Ka-who? Ka-what?" Garrett whispered to Randi.

Randi shrugged.

"Or maybe Mr. C. will just let Barry Kuda deal with the two of you," the hotel worker went on.

"And who's that?" Randi squeaked again.

"Mr. C.'s assistant," he answered. "He handles public relations. Now move it," he ordered, ripping the life vests from their backs as he shoved them up the beach. "Before I take a bite out of you myself."

"Geez, oh, man," Garrett mumbled under his breath. "They take this Nanuwee feast pretty seriously around here."

"Tell me about it," Randi shot back as they headed toward the pavilion where the stick-clapping rehearsals were going on.

All around the property, dozens of other rehearsals were taking place as well. Every guest at the resort seemed to be stuck in some kind of class for Nanuwee night. There were fire-dancing and torch-tossing classes for men; hula and streamer-twirling for women. There was shell-blowing and drumbeating. But none seemed quite as boring as the class Randi and Garrett were headed for.

"Oh, great," Garrett grumbled as they reached the stick-clapping pavilion. "That goofy Farkle kid is here again today."

"What goofy Farkle kid?" Randi asked.

"Bobby Farkle," Garrett said, pointing to a roly-poly boy in a polka-dot bathing suit. He was covered from head to toe in neon lime-colored sunblock.

"Oh, him," Randi said, recognizing the Farkle kid right away. "He almost poked my eye out yesterday with his stick," she told Garrett.

"Yeah, well, he smacked the Jimbo kid right in the face and gave him a nosebleed." Garrett pointed to another boy who was sitting next to Bobby Farkle. He was a tenth the size of the Farkle kid, but just as goofy. Instead of gobs of sunblock, he was wearing a big straw hat, a long-sleeved beach cover-up that zipped to his chin, and Bermuda shorts that hung down practically to his ankles. "I'm telling you, we're the only normal kids in this group," Garrett whispered.

Randi hated to admit it, but she agreed. The stick-clapping class was jam-packed with lulus.

"You're late!" the instructor growled at Randi and Garrett. "Does Mr. C. know about this?" he asked.

Randi and Garrett shook their heads.

"Well, he will," the instructor snapped. "Now pick up

your sticks and take a seat before Mr. C. and Mr. Kuda take a pound of my flesh for not having you under control."

One thing was clear. When it came to Nanuwee rehearsals, Paradise was torture.

Randi scrambled to pick up a pair of bamboo sticks. Garrett did the same.

"From now on, the two of you will be partners," the instructor told them.

Garrett smiled from ear to ear as he and Randi found a seat. "Yesterday, I had Jimbo Traytor," he whispered to Randi. "At least we'll get to be together for the next couple of days."

Randi smiled back. She was relieved too. The day before, she'd been paired with Bobby Farkle's sister, Franny, who spent most of practice sticking the bamboo sticks up her nose.

"You all know how important it is that we get things right for the Feast of Nanuwee," the instructor said. "And while we need more work on our stick clapping, today we'll be learning the Feast of Nanuwee song as well."

"Terrific," Garrett grumbled. "We've got to sing too?"

Randi just sighed.

"Repeat after me," the instructor began. "Ama lama, kooma lama, kooma lama, beast day."

Immediately, the group did as they were told. Except for Randi and Garrett, who started to snicker.

"'I'm a lama'?" Randi laughed. "What the heck does that mean?"

Garrett didn't answer.

Another voice did. "It means you are the servant of the great spirit of Nanuwee."

Randi looked up to see a tall, well-built man in an expensive-looking white suit. His jet-black hair was slicked back with grease, and he wore dark sunglasses. Randi could see her face reflected in the lenses as she stared up at him.

Alongside that man was a much shorter, mean-looking guy, dressed in a charcoal-gray suit. Above his beady black eyes was a single white eyebrow that ran straight across his forehead. His nose was as crooked as a boxer's, and his jaw stuck out so far, his bottom teeth were showing. On his lapel was a silver name tag. It read "B. Kuda."

Both men were glaring down at Randi and Garrett.

"Mr. Carcharias," the instructor said, bowing his head respectfully. "Welcome to our class."

The tall man with the sunglasses nodded back.

"Class," the instructor continued, sounding a bit nervous, "this is Mr. Carcharodon Carcharias, owner of this wonderful resort, and founder of Paradise."

"Please," Mr. Carcharias said. "Just call me Mr. C. And this is Mr. Kuda," he went on. "My assistant and head of public relations."

"How ya doing, Mr. C.?" Bobby Farkle shouted from the group as his sister, Franny, shoved the bamboo stick back up her nose.

"Just fine," Mr. C. answered. "The real question is, how are *you* all doing? The Feast of Nanuwee is a very important affair here at Paradise. And we want all our guests to perform their very best." He glared at Randi and Garrett again. "It's important to me. Isn't that right, Mr. Kuda?"

Mr. Kuda nodded.

"Well, we've just started to learn the song for the feast, Mr. C.," the instructor told him. "But we're coming along with our stick clapping. Aren't we, class?"

"Wonderful," Mr. C. said. "I'd like to see a demonstration, pair by pair."

Randi shot Garrett a worried look. For the life of her, she didn't remember the rhythm they'd learned the day before. She had been too grossed out by Franny Farkle to pay attention. And judging by the look on Garrett's face, he didn't remember either.

Luckily, Jimbo Traytor started waving his hand in the air. "Oooh, oooh," he grunted. "Pick me and Bobby first!"

"Fine," the instructor said, waving them up to Mr. C. "Bobby Farkle and Jimmy Traytor will go first."

"My friends call me Jimbo," Jimmy Traytor told Mr. C. as he and Bobby got ready to clap sticks.

Randi watched as Jimbo and Bobby started banging their sticks together like maniacs in a rhythm she didn't recognize at all.

Neither did the instructor. But before he could get them to stop, Jimbo whacked his thumb so hard, he started to wail. And Bobby was swinging his arms around so enthusiastically, he knocked Mr. C.'s sunglasses right off his face.

They went sailing straight into Randi's lap.

"My glasses!" Mr. C. growled, raising his hand to his face as if he were trying to shield his eyes from the sun.

Randi lifted the glasses from her lap and held them up to Mr. C. "Here they are," she said.

"Thank you," Mr. C. replied. His thin, pale lips curled into a grin.

Randi caught only a glimpse of Mr. C.'s eyes before he quickly replaced his glasses. Still, she saw enough to make her shiver.

The eyes Mr. C. seemed so eager to shield were bright yellow with little black slits in them, like a cat's. Stranger still were his eyelids. They weren't on the tops of his eyes. They were on the bottom.

Carcharodon Carcharias blinked up—just like a fish.

CHAPTER 5

As Mr. C. turned back to the instructor, Randi nudged Garrett in the ribs. "Did you see that?" she asked in a whisper. "Did you see that guy's eyes?"

Garrett shook his head.

"They were like a cat's eyes," Randi told him. "Only they blinked like a fish."

"Yeah, right." Garrett laughed. "And the guy on the beach had duck feet."

Randi sighed. Garrett didn't believe a word she was saying.

Mr. C. sighed too. "I'm not at all pleased with the progress here," he told the instructor. "From now on, we will start our days with Nanuwee rehearsals, at eight A.M. Each class will continue until ten. There will be no other activities in the morning. No swimming, no sailing, no golfing. And no Sea-Dooing," he added, looking down at Randi and Garrett.

"What about breakfast?" Bobby Farkle whined. "Can't we even have breakfast? If I don't eat breakfast, I get sick."

"Then you'll have to get up extra early to feed, won't you?" Mr. Kuda said, looming over Bobby. "That's what I do."

"Come, Mr. Kuda," Mr. C. said, tugging Mr. Kuda away from Bobby Farkle. "We have work to do. Dismiss this class for the day," he told the instructor. "We'll whip them into shape tomorrow."

With that, Mr. C. and Mr. Kuda turned and headed for the main lobby of the resort.

"This Nanuwee thing is out of control," Garrett told Randi as the class started to scatter. "The brochure said it was supposed to be some kind of luau. But it's more like military boot camp."

"For real," Randi agreed. "It's way too weird." *And so are all the people who work here,* she thought. But she didn't say it to Garrett.

"So what do you want to do now?" Garrett asked as they headed across the property. "Want to go back down to the beach?"

Randi shook her head. No way did she want to go back in that water.

"I didn't think so," Garrett said.

"Have you been to the Dolphin Encounter yet?" Randi asked.

"No," Garrett said. "I didn't even know there was one."

"It's down past the shark lagoon," Randi told him. "You can get there through the tunnels or over the rope bridge. I wanted to go yesterday," she added, "but it was only open in the morning and I got there too late. It's supposed to be open all day today."

"Do you get to swim with a dolphin?" Garrett asked.

"I don't think so," Randi answered. "But you get to feed one and pet him."

"Cool!" Garrett exclaimed. "Let's do it!"

"You want to take the rope bridge?" Randi asked.

"Sure," Garrett answered. "I love that thing."

The two of them took off running. The rope bridge was suspended in midair from wooden beams that were anchored on opposite sides of the shark lagoon. It was so high up, Randi and Garrett could see most of the property as they crossed over it.

"Hey, look," Randi said, pointing out to the beach. "I think I see my parents."

Garrett followed her finger. "Are they the ones headed for the volleyball game with that guy in the blue trunks and that lady with the green T-shirt?" he asked.

"Yeah," Randi said. "That's them."

"Well, guess what?" he said. "The other two are my parents."

"You're kidding!" Randi laughed.

"Nope," Garrett said. "It looks like they're having a fun time together."

"Good," Randi told him. "Maybe we'll get to sit together

at dinner tonight so that neither of us gets stuck with the Farkles or the Traytors."

"Let's hope so," Garrett said.

"Speaking of the Farkles," Randi said as they reached the end of the rope bridge, "look who's heading to the Dolphin Encounter too."

Below them, Bobby and Franny Farkle were emerging from the tunnel, with Jimbo Traytor and his dad right behind them. Bobby, Franny, and Jimbo were goofy enough, but Jimbo's dad definitely won the prize. Mr. Traytor was the only guy Randi had ever seen who wore a bow tie with his bathing suit, not to mention black, knee-high socks with his brown strap-on sandals.

"Not for real," Garrett groaned at the sight. "Do you want to just skip it?" he asked Randi.

Randi thought about it for a second. "Nah," she said. She wanted to see a dolphin much more than she wanted to avoid the Farkles and the Traytors.

As soon as Randi set foot on the pier that led to the dolphin lagoon, her adrenaline started to pump. Dolphins were just about her favorite mammals on earth, and she couldn't wait to touch one.

In the distance, she saw a dolphin leap from the water and propel himself across the surface standing on his tail.

"Garrett, look!" Randi squealed with delight. "There's the dolphin! Come on!"

Randi ran down the rest of the pier, with Garrett right behind her.

The Farkles and Traytors were already standing with

the dolphin trainer. The dolphin was back underwater, nowhere in sight.

"Okay," the trainer said, looking at his watch. "Let's get this over with."

"Boy," Garrett whispered to Randi. "He's not very friendly, is he?"

Randi laughed.

"So how many of us are there?" the trainer asked as he started counting heads. "Six?"

"Seven, if you're counting yourself," Jimbo's dad pointed out.

"I don't count myself," the trainer snapped back. "I only count guests. And I'd like to get this show on the road. Okay, everybody," he said. "Into the water."

"We get to swim with the dolphin?" Franny Farkle shrieked excitedly.

"No," the trainer answered. "You get to feed him and pat him on his slimy fat head."

"For a dolphin trainer, he doesn't seem too fond of dolphins, does he?" Randi whispered to Garrett.

"Now, everybody get in the water," the trainer ordered. "Just jump right in. And don't worry, it'll only come up to your waists. Except for the guy with the bow tie. It might be up to your neck," he told Mr. Traytor.

Randi and Garrett exchanged amused looks as they jumped into the dolphin pool. Mr. Traytor really was pretty short.

When everyone was in the water, the trainer sat down on the ledge of the pool and patted the surface of the water with his hand. "This is how I call the dolphin," he said. "He hears the vibrations and then he comes."

Two seconds later, Randi watched as the most beautiful creature she'd ever seen swam toward the group.

"Just stay still, everybody," the trainer instructed, jumping into the water himself. "I'll introduce you."

The dolphin swam right up to Randi and lifted his head out of the water.

Randi's heart felt as if it were going to burst. Never in her life had she experienced anything so magical, so wonderful. There she was, standing just inches away from a dolphin, who was staring right back at her with the biggest, most beautiful eyes she'd ever seen. Eyes that seemed just as human as her own.

"Eeeeeee-eeeeeee-eeeeeee!" The dolphin opened his mouth and made a kind of clicking sound.

"He's talking to me!" Randi exclaimed, laughing with glee. "Look, Garrett! He's talking to me!"

"He's not talking to *you*," Bobby Farkle huffed. "He's talking to all of us."

"What's his name?" Randi asked the trainer, ignoring Bobby.

"Milo," the trainer answered. "His name is Milo."

"Can I touch him?" Randi asked.

"Sure," the trainer answered. "Just keep your hand away from his blow hole. They get pretty testy about that."

Randi reached out to pat Milo's snout. She was expecting it to feel kind of slimy. But it didn't. In fact, it felt almost dry, and smooth—and wonderful!

Jimbo Traytor reached out to touch Milo too. But Milo quickly pulled his head underwater.

"Hey!" Jimbo complained to the trainer. "I want to touch him too!"

The trainer rolled his eyes. "I'll tell you what, kid," he said. "You can do better than touch him. You can feed him a sardine. How's that?"

"What about us?" Bobby and Franny whined.

"You can all feed him one," the trainer said. He reached up onto the pier and grabbed a bucket of dead fish. "Here you go," he said, handing them out. "Now, you can either hand your fish to Milo, or you can get him to give you a kiss."

"What do you mean?" Randi asked.

"Well, if you put the tail in your teeth and let the rest of the fish dangle from your lips, Milo will come right up to your face and take it from you," the trainer explained. "Then you can get yourself a slimy little dolphin kiss."

Garrett went first, opting for the kiss. Sure enough, Milo took the fish from his lips.

"Too cool!" Garrett exclaimed. "You have to do it, Randi."

Randi wasn't too thrilled about putting a dead fish tail between her teeth, but she *was* thrilled about Milo. Besides, she would do anything to tell her friends back home that she got to "kiss" a real dolphin. So she took a deep breath, bit down on the tail, and patted the water for Milo to come.

Within seconds, Randi and Milo were nose-to-nose. He gently took the fish from her lips. It really did feel like a kiss. "He did it!" Randi beamed. "He really did it!"

"My turn!" Jimbo Traytor insisted, cramming the fish into his mouth. But when he patted the water, Milo swam the other way.

"Hey!" Jimbo protested through clenched teeth. "How come he's not kissing me? They got to kiss him! And if they got to kiss him, I want to kiss him too!"

Jimbo tried to suck in some air so he could keep on whining. But he sucked in the dead sardine instead.

"Ew, gross!" Franny Farkle cried. "He just ate that slimy dead fish!"

"I'm gonna die, aren't I, Dad?" Jimbo Traytor started to panic. He was gagging and spitting and wiping his tongue with his T-shirt. He even stuck his finger down his throat to try to make himself throw up.

"He's going to get botulism or something," Franny said, adding to the hysteria.

"What kind of a resort is this?" Mr. Traytor barked at the trainer. "How could you allow children to put dead fish in their mouths? This is unforgivable," he continued to rant as Jimbo continued to gag. "In fact, it may be against the law. I'm an attorney, you know. I just may sue you!"

With that, Mr. Traytor grabbed Jimbo and pulled him out of the Dolphin Encounter. The two of them stormed away, with Bobby and Franny Farkle right on their heels.

Randi and Garrett cracked up.

So did Milo the dolphin. Or at least it sounded that

way, because suddenly he was *"eee-eee-ing"* like crazy.

Garrett was about to reach out and pet him when the trainer barked, "That's it! Show's over. I've had enough aggravation for one day. Now get out of the water."

"I guess we'd better do what he says," Garrett said. Then he looked at Milo. "You really are a cool fish, you know?"

Milo shook his head as if he understood. But he wasn't shaking it yes; he was shaking it no. Randi reached out to sneak one last touch. As her fingers made contact with the dolphin, something very strange happened.

"Tell him I'm not a fish!" Milo said to Randi.

Randi jumped back. "Oh, my gosh!" she gasped. "The dolphin just talked to me!"

CHAPTER 6

"You're out of your mind," Garrett said, looking at Randi as if she were bonkers. "There's no way that dolphin talked."

"Didn't you hear him?" Randi asked. Her heart was still pounding.

"I heard him," the trainer said.

Relief washed over Randi. She wasn't crazy. The dolphin really had spoken to her.

"He said, *'eee-eee-eee,'*" the trainer told her, imitating the sound that dolphins make.

Randi looked at Garrett, who was staring at her with disbelief. Then she looked at Milo, whose head was still above the water, his eyes focused intently on her. "I'm telling you, he spoke English," she said weakly. "He told me to tell you he's not a fish."

"Yeah, right." Garrett laughed.

"He did." She said it so quietly that even she barely heard the sound of her own voice.

"Okay, you two," the trainer said. "Out of the water. This dolphin encounter is over." He waved his hand at Milo as if to shoo him away.

Milo continued to look at Randi.

"Go!" the trainer said gruffly, shooing Milo again.

"Eee-eee-eee," Milo said, nodding his head at Randi. Then he dove underwater and swam away.

Garrett lifted himself out of the water onto the wooden dock. "So if dolphins aren't fish," he asked the trainer, "what are they?"

"A pain in my butt," the trainer shot back.

"They're mammals," Randi said. "Gentle, kind mammals. And they're just as smart as we are."

"Don't kid yourself, little girl," the trainer told her. "Dolphins just pretend to be gentle. They're really wild animals. Sometimes they can even be dangerous to people. You don't want to get near a dolphin unless you're with an experienced trainer like me."

Randi climbed up onto the dock and began following Garrett and the trainer away from the dolphin area. She kept looking over her shoulder, hoping to see Milo again. But there was no sign of him anymore.

You are totally weird, she told herself. *How could you think that a dolphin just talked to you?*

But another part of Randi was absolutely certain of what she'd heard. And something told her that the dolphin trainer suspected she was telling the truth too. He certainly hadn't laughed at her, the way Garrett had.

"*Now* what do you want to do?" Garrett asked as they wandered down the pier and the trainer headed off in the other direction, toward the office.

Randi stopped walking and shrugged. "I don't know," she said. But she did know. She wanted to go back to the dock. She wanted to see Milo again. And suddenly she realized that she had an excuse to do just that. "I left my sandals down on the dock," she told Garrett. "I have to go back and get them."

"Hurry up," he told her. "I'll wait here for you."

Randi took off down the pier.

Her sandals were lying on the wooden platform right where she'd left them before she'd gotten into the water. As she bent down to pick them up, her eyes scanned the water, looking for any sign of the dolphin. "Milo?" she said softly.

There was no reply.

Finally, Randi snatched up her sandals and turned to leave. But a sudden splash in the water made her turn back.

"*Eee-eee-eee!*" Milo was right there, close enough to touch.

Dolphins can be dangerous to people.

The trainer's words echoed in Randi's head. She didn't want to believe that. She wanted to kneel down and pet Milo again. But now she was afraid.

"You did talk to me before, didn't you?" she asked,

looking into Milo's warm, gentle eyes.

Milo nodded his head. *"Eee-eee-eee."*

"Talk to me again," Randi pleaded.

"Eee-eee-eee," was all Milo said.

"I must be crazy." Randi shook her head.

Milo moved closer to the platform, as close as he could get. He was right at Randi's feet. *"Eee-eee-eee."* It sounded as though he were pleading with her.

Slowly, cautiously, Randi knelt down. She reached out her hand and touched Milo gently.

"Hey!" a voice snarled. "What are you doing down there?"

Randi glanced over her shoulder to see the trainer glaring at her from the path above the dock.

"Get away from that dolphin," he growled.

But before Randi could withdraw her hand, Milo spoke to her again. "Don't let that imbecile know that I'm talking to you." Milo's strange, gravelly voice was urgent but clear. "It will only make your situation worse. You must come back tonight after dark, when it's safe for us to meet," he said. "But remember, there's danger all around you."

CHAPTER 7

Randi wasn't about to tell the trainer a thing. And she wasn't about to tell Garrett what had happened either. She didn't want to tell anyone. Who would believe her? Everybody knew that dolphins couldn't talk—everybody but Randi.

"There's danger all around you," Milo had said. What did that mean?

The only way to find out was to go back after dark. But Randi didn't want to go alone. She was too afraid. She would have to find a way to ask Garrett to go with her.

All day long she struggled to bring it up without sounding completely insane. She was so preoccupied with her problem that she didn't have any fun on the beach, or at the pool, or even in the arcade.

By dinnertime, she'd given up on the idea of talking to Garrett about it. She sat at the table in the grand dining room with her parents and Garrett and his parents, trying to put the whole thing out of her mind.

But she couldn't do it. *"There's danger all around you."* Milo's words kept repeating in her head.

Randi's brain raced from one weird image to the next— the duck feet on the beach, Mr. C.'s creepy eyes, a talking dolphin! Something fishy was going on in Paradise.

Suddenly, Randi felt a cold, clammy hand close down around her shoulder. It startled her so badly, she jumped.

"Are you enjoying your stay with us?" a voice behind her inquired.

Randi looked up to see Mr. C. standing over her, smiling down at the group.

Mr. Kuda was with him. Randi had seen the two of them earlier, making their way around the dining room, stopping at every table to chitchat with the guests. But she hadn't seen them sneak up on her.

"Oh, yes," Randi's mother replied. "We're having a lovely time."

"It's the nicest vacation I've ever had," Garrett's mother agreed.

"You call this a vacation?" Mr. Traytor, who was sitting at the next table, butted in. "This place is a hazard. Why, today my boy Jimbo here nearly choked on a sardine. And I set my bow tie on fire while I was practicing torch tossing for this Feast of Nanuwee nonsense. If I weren't here for free, I'd have left the island already."

"I'm sorry if you have suffered any inconvenience," Mr. C. apologized to Mr. Traytor.

"Inconvenience?" Mr. Traytor snapped back. "Do you

realize that I could sue this resort for what's happened to us?"

"I hope you won't do that," Mr. C. said. "I promise we will do everything we can to make the rest of your stay as pleasant as possible."

But things only got more *un*pleasant.

The Farkles, who were sharing the table with the Traytors, wanted to take a picture of their children with Mr. C. and Mr. Kuda.

"Please don't," Mr. C. said as Mr. Farkle pulled out his camera. "My eyes are very sensitive to light. That's why I always wear dark glasses. I'm afraid the flash would cause me great—"

But before Mr. C. could finish the sentence, Mr. Farkle had snapped the picture.

Mr. C.'s hands shot up to his face and he groaned in pain.

"You idiot," Mr. Kuda snarled. He knocked the camera out of Mr. Farkle's hands, then lifted his foot and brought the heel of his shoe crashing down onto the camera, smashing it to smithereens. For an instant, Randi thought he was going to do the same thing to Mr. Farkle.

"It's okay, Barry," Mr. C. said, putting his hand on Mr. Kuda's arm to calm him. "No harm done."

"No harm done?" Mr. Traytor shouted. "Look at what your goon just did to that camera! Do you have any idea what a camera like that costs?"

"I will get Mr. Farkle a new camera," Mr. C. assured them, "a better camera. Now, if you will please excuse me."

Without another word, Mr. C. turned and headed out of

the dining room, with Mr. Kuda right behind him.

There was silence as every guest watched them go. But once they were gone, the room broke into nervous whispers.

Randi was feeling pretty nervous herself. Mr. Kuda wasn't exactly acting like the host with the most. In fact, he was kind of scary. Still, Randi had no desire to share her feelings with the rest of the table. Nor did she want to sit around listening to the adults, who had returned to making pleasant chitchat. Besides, she'd already finished her dinner and so had Garrett. "May we be excused?" she asked.

"I don't see why not," her father said. "Where are you going?"

"I don't know." Randi shrugged.

"Want to go to the arcade?" Garrett suggested.

"Sure," Randi answered.

"Be back in the room by ten o'clock," Randi's mother told her.

"Okay," Randi said as she and Garrett headed out of the dining room.

"You want to go through the tunnel under the lagoon before we go to the arcade?" Garrett asked. "It's really cool at night."

"Sure," Randi agreed again.

They made their way down the hallway toward the exit that put them on the pathway to the tunnels. Garrett was about to push open the door when Randi stopped him.

"Listen," she whispered.

Angry voices drifted out from behind a closed door down the hall.

"I want that Traytor guy and his kid out of here!" It was Mr. C.'s voice, no doubt about it.

Randi and Garrett exchanged glances. Garrett took a step in the direction from which the voices were coming and gestured for Randi to follow him.

Silently, they crept along the wall, listening as the complaints about the Traytors continued to filter through the door.

"They're big trouble, boss." Mr. Kuda was talking now.

"I don't want them at the Feast of Nanuwee." It was Mr. C. again. "They're sure to make a mess of it. And we can't afford to let that happen."

"Yeah." It was another voice now. "That Jimbo kid is as dumb as chum."

Randi had to put her hand over her mouth to stop herself from laughing at the way they were talking about Mr. Traytor and his goofy kid.

As Randi and Garrett moved closer, Randi saw that the door was slightly ajar. Cautiously, she and Garrett peeked inside. A dozen men, all in suits, were seated around a large round table.

The room looked like Mr. C.'s private dining room.

"So who gets to do the dirty deed?" the man directly across from Mr. C. asked.

"I couldn't care less," Mr. C. answered. "Just see to it that the Traytors are gone by morning."

Randi and Garrett looked at each other, confused and

a little concerned. Neither one of them liked the Traytors, but Mr. C.'s decision seemed a bit harsh.

When Randi looked back into the room, she saw Mr. C. reach for the fancy crystal goblet on the table in front of him. "Cheers!" he said as he raised the goblet into the air.

Randi stood frozen in horror.

The goblet was full of a clear liquid that looked like plain water—and there was a goldfish swimming around inside it!

"To the great spirit, Nanuwee!" Mr. C. made a toast. Then he downed the contents of his glass in one gulp—goldfish and all.

Randi's stomach lurched. She was about to turn away when Garrett pointed out another repulsive sight.

A waitress stood beside Mr. C., ladling what looked like bloody guts into his soup bowl.

"The chef prepared this specially for you," the waitress told Mr. C. "It was brought over from a nearby island."

Mr. C. dipped his spoon into the bowl and stirred the disgusting contents. "Wonderful!" he sighed. "I can't wait to taste it. But first, an appetizer." He reached for a silver dome that covered a plate in the center of the table.

Randi nearly fainted when Mr. C. lifted the dome.

Under it were dozens of slimy black eels, curled into a giant, slithering, pulsating knot.

Mr. C. stuck his hand into the mess and pulled out the biggest, fattest eel of the bunch. Then he threw back his head, opened his mouth, and slid the slimy creature down his throat.

CHAPTER 8

"Gross!" Randi cried as she watched the eel slither down Mr. C.'s throat.

Garrett quickly clamped his hand over Randi's mouth before she could make any more noise. The last thing they needed to do was attract the attention of the strange and scary men inside the private dining room.

A sudden beeping sound made both Randi and Garrett jump. They quickly plastered themselves against the wall behind the door.

"I've got to go," Mr. Kuda said as the beeping stopped. "My twelve hours are up."

"Wait a minute." Mr. C. stopped him. "I want you to be sure to take care of that Traytor problem."

"It will be done," Mr. Kuda assured him. "I really have to go now."

But Mr. C. kept right on talking. "The Feast of Nanuwee must be perfect. There can be no mistakes. We don't get a second chance."

"I understand," Mr. Kuda said, sounding very nervous. "May I please go now?"

There was no answer to the question.

Desperately, Randi pointed to the exit down the hall. But before either she or Garrett could make a run for it, the door to the dining room flew open.

Randi and Garrett were hidden behind the door, frozen in terror. *We're sure to be caught now,* Randi thought. *As soon as somebody closes this door again, they'll see us.*

Randi held her breath as the footsteps moved away from them, heading for the door that led to the outside. Meanwhile, the door to the dining room stayed open and Randi and Garrett stayed put.

Before Randi could even begin to think of what they should do next, the door began to close. Someone from inside the room must have reached out to close it—without looking behind it.

"Whew," Randi sighed. She and Garrett were safe. But it had been a close call—too close for Randi.

"Let's get out of here," she whispered. She didn't even wait for Garrett to agree before she started running for the door to the outside.

Garrett was right behind her.

"What was that all about?" he said once they'd gotten outside.

"I don't know," Randi said. All she could think about

was the ominous warning Milo had given her: *"There's danger all around you."* Randi had to make Garrett believe that Milo had spoken. "Listen," she started. "Remember when—"

But Garrett interrupted her. "Look!" he said, pointing down the pathway ahead of them. It was the pathway that led to the shark lagoon.

Randi saw Mr. Kuda racing toward the tunnels. As he ran through the circle of light cast by one of the many torches that lit the path, something strange began happening to him.

The back of his suit jacket had ripped apart, and a sharp silvery object was sticking out through the tear. At the same time, the color of his skin seemed to be swiftly changing to a shimmering gray.

Randi blinked hard. "This is too weird," she said. "What the heck is happening to him?"

"I don't know," Garrett answered. "Let's follow him and find out," he said, grabbing Randi's arm and pulling her along.

Mr. Kuda tore off his jacket as he ducked into the tunnel. A spiny ridge stuck out of the back of his shirt.

It looks like a fin! Randi realized with horror.

She pulled back as they reached the tunnel. "I don't know, Garrett . . . maybe we shouldn't follow him."

But Garrett was insistent. "We'll stay a safe distance back," he assured her. "Come on!"

Inside the tunnel, Randi could hear Mr. Kuda's footsteps echoing up ahead. He was still moving fast. But the tunnel curved, and they couldn't see him anymore. The two of them followed the sound of his footsteps, trying to be as quiet as they could as they ran to keep up.

Around them, the sharks swam close to the Plexiglas, keeping the same pace as Randi and Garrett. But Randi was too freaked out by Mr. Kuda to pay them any attention.

Suddenly, she and Garrett came to a place where the tunnel split in two directions.

"He went that way," Garrett whispered, nodding to the right.

They began to run again.

Here the tunnel was straight enough for Randi to see Mr. Kuda ahead of them. But she caught only a glimpse of him before he made a sharp turn around another corner.

When Randi and Garrett got to the place where Mr. Kuda had turned, they both stopped running.

The Plexiglas tunnel ended. The walls were made of stone and looked like the inside of a cave.

There, at the end, was a door through which Mr. Kuda had disappeared, slamming it shut behind him. But he'd slammed it with such force, it had bounced open just a crack.

Garrett started moving toward the door.

"Where are you going?" Randi grabbed at the back of his shirt to stop him.

"I just want to take a peek," he whispered back.

Randi knew it was a bad idea, but she crept down the hallway after Garrett anyway.

There was no sound coming from behind the door. Randi wondered if there was a room back there, or more secret tunnels.

They were about to find out.

Garrett reached the door and pressed his eye against the crack. The moment he did, Randi could see the blood drain from his face.

What? she mouthed the word in a panic. But Garrett didn't look at her—even when she shoved him in the ribs. Randi had no choice but to look for herself.

When she did, her heart started pounding even harder than it already was.

CHAPTER 9

Behind the door was a cavelike chamber that looked like a control room. Through the crack, Randi could see dozens of TV monitors lining the walls. Each one showed a different area of the resort. On one screen, Randi saw the lobby of the hotel, buzzing with guests; on another, the main restaurant. She could even see the pools and the tennis courts. What she couldn't see was Mr. Kuda.

Garrett pushed the door open a little bit farther.

Randi's heart nearly exploded when the squeak that it made echoed throughout the tunnels. She was sure that Mr. Kuda would slither out of the shadows in the room at any moment to grab them.

But all they saw of Mr. Kuda were his shredded shirt and his shoes, lying in the middle of the floor.

"Where the heck did he go?" Garrett asked as he and Randi stepped cautiously inside.

"I don't know," Randi answered. Her eyes darted around the room, searching for another door. But the only other opening she could see was a circular vault in the wall that looked like a submarine porthole.

"I didn't see him come out of here," Garrett gulped. "Did you?"

What kind of stupid question was that?

"I think I definitely would have noticed that," Randi snapped. "Especially since he would have been walking out with a fin on his back!" she practically shouted. "Not to mention the fact that he was turning silver!"

"Oh, man!" Garrett cringed. "Something really weird is going on around here!"

"I've been trying to tell you that all day!" Randi said.

"So what do you think this room is?" Garrett wondered, looking up at the monitors.

"I don't know," Randi answered again. "It looks like some kind of surveillance room. And from the looks of it, they have cameras set up all over the place. Even in the guest rooms!" Randi pointed to one of the monitors above the desk that stood against the far wall. On the screen were Bobby and Franny Farkle, sitting on the bed in their room watching a movie. Bobby was shoveling down a giant sundae, and Franny was digging for something up her nose.

"Check it out," Garrett told Randi. "There's a keyboard with all the room numbers on it. There are keys for every location on the property. It looks like you can punch up anyplace you want to see."

"Hit my room," Randi said. "It's 426."

Garrett scanned the keyboard down the row of 400s. The moment he pushed 426, Randi's room came up on the monitor overhead. Randi could see the mess she'd left just before dinner. Her clothes were strewn all over the place.

"I can't believe they're watching us all the time," Randi gasped.

"Me neither." Garrett looked shaken. "But why?"

"I'm not sure," Randi said, noticing sound knobs on the monitors. "But something tells me they're *listening* to us too." She twisted the knob on the Farkles' monitor.

"Buuuuuuuurrrrrrrrppppppp." The sound of Bobby Farkle belching was the first thing they heard.

"That was a good one." Franny Farkle laughed. "Do it again."

"From which end?" Bobby asked.

Randi quickly turned the sound down. There was no way she wanted to listen to that. And she didn't want to see it either. Her eyes quickly moved to another monitor— one that nearly stopped her heart.

On the screen was the dolphin pool. And there, by the dock, was Milo. He was up on his tail so that his body was out of the water. And he was scanning the pier as if he were searching for something, or some*one*!

"Oh, my gosh," Randi gasped. "He's waiting for me!"

"Who?" Garrett asked. "Who's waiting for you?"

"Milo," Randi replied, pointing to the screen.

"The dolphin?" Garrett said, sounding confused.

Randi nodded.

"What makes you think he's waiting for you?" Garrett asked.

Randi swallowed hard. "He told me to come back tonight after dark," she blurted out. "He also told me there was danger all around us."

Garrett stared at her. "I thought you said Milo told you he wasn't a fish," he shot back.

At least he's not laughing, Randi thought. "He did," she told Garrett. "But when I went back to the pier to get my sandals, he talked to me again. I know it sounds weird," she went on, "but I'm telling you, it's true."

"Then let's go talk to him," Garrett said.

"You believe me?" Randi asked.

Garrett nodded. "There's so much other weird stuff going on around here, why shouldn't I believe in a talking fish?"

Randi smiled. "He's not—"

"I know, I know." Garrett cut her off. "He's not a fish."

"Come on," Randi said. "Let's go."

Randi and Garrett stepped quietly out of the control room back into the Plexiglas tunnel under the shark lagoon. Luckily, there was no one in sight. The tunnel was deserted.

"This way," Randi whispered as she headed to the left. "This will lead us out to the pier."

As the two of them made their way toward the exit, Randi suddenly sensed that they were being followed. Over her shoulder, she could see a pair of beady black eyes staring at them and silvery-black jaws starting to part, exposing dozens of razor-sharp teeth.

58

Randi stopped quickly.

So did the barracuda behind the glass. In fact, its lean, sleek body was perfectly still. But the glare in its eyes was murderous.

Randi shivered as her mind flashed back to the shark feeder with the long, jagged scar down his face. Hadn't he been attacked by a vicious barracuda?

"What's the matter?" Garrett demanded.

"Nothing," Randi lied. It was enough that she had gotten Garrett to believe in a "talking fish." She wasn't about to try to convince him that they were being followed by a barracuda.

They started moving forward again.

So did the barracuda.

Randi kept her eyes straight ahead. She didn't want to look at the fish—until Garrett pointed it out too.

"I know you're going to think I'm insane," he told her. "But I think this barracuda is following us."

"Me too!" Randi exclaimed.

"He's one mean-looking sucker, isn't he?" Garrett said, as he moved closer to the glass to examine the barracuda's face.

"For real," Randi agreed as the barracuda glared at Garrett. "I'm just glad he's behind that glass."

Suddenly, the barracuda shot to the surface of the water with the speed of a bullet.

"Guess we must have spooked him," Garrett said.

"Good," Randi responded. "Because he definitely spooked me." They started to move on again.

But before they'd taken even a step, the barracuda was back. Only now it had a couple of friends along—two fearsome-looking sharks. They were swimming on opposite sides of the barracuda.

Randi quickly picked up her pace.

So did the barracuda and its buddies.

Even the glass that separated Randi and Garrett from the three killers wasn't enough to make Randi feel safe. Not anymore. She ran to the end of the tunnel, with Garrett right beside her.

The moment they reached the outside, Randi didn't bother looking back. She ran straight for the pier to see Milo, sure that she was leaving the sharks and barracuda behind.

"Do you see him?" Garrett asked as he followed Randi down the planks that led to the Dolphin Encounter.

The torches in the distance provided hardly enough light to see anything clearly. But as Randi scanned the water below, there wasn't even a shadow to be seen. "No," she sighed, finally reaching the dock. "I don't see him anywhere."

"Maybe he got tired of waiting," Garrett suggested.

Randi hoped not. "Milo?" she called out.

The water was still.

"Pat it," Garrett said. "That's how the trainer guy got him to come, remember?"

"Good idea," Randi agreed. She got down on her knees on the wooden dock and patted the surface of the water.

The outline of a fin appeared in the distance.

"Look," Garrett exclaimed. "He's coming."

"Yes!" Randi punched the air triumphantly. But as the

fin cut through the water, moving closer, she realized that something was wrong.

The fin was too big to be Milo's. It looked like the one Randi had seen in the sea.

A second fin surfaced.

These weren't dolphin fins! They were shark fins!

Within seconds, the two fins were moving side by side, speeding toward the dock like a couple of missiles.

"Sharks!" Randi cried.

Just then, something else surfaced in the water. A silvery-black head popped up between the two shark fins. Its black, beady eyes fixed their glare on Randi.

"Holy smokes!" Garrett shouted. "It's sharks *and* a barracuda!"

Randi gulped. It wasn't just any barracuda. It was the same one that had been following them in the tunnels! She was sure of it. But now the barracuda and its shark friends weren't simply following them—they were coming at them with a vengeance.

"Let's get out of here!" Garrett said, reaching out to pull Randi to her feet.

But before he'd even taken hold of her arm, a terrible jolt hit the dock. Beneath their feet, the wood broke apart as if someone had set off a stick of dynamite.

In a split second Randi realized that the sharks had rammed the pier, hard. As they did it again, splintered boards flew up in the air, landing *splat* in the shark-infested water.

And so did Randi and Garrett.

CHAPTER

10

Black water swirled around Randi, sucking her under. She struggled to cling to Garrett, who was thrashing about, desperately trying to grab the small clump of wood that was all that was left of the dock.

Ten feet behind them, the two black fins surfaced again.

Terror made Randi's heart race. For a moment, she almost wished she would just pass out and sink to the bottom of the lagoon. At least then she wouldn't feel herself being ripped to shreds by bloodthirsty sharks, or nibbled to pieces by a flesh-eating barracuda.

"Randi!" Garrett had managed to grab hold of the remains of the dock. "Come on!"

Randi started to swim forward as Garrett hoisted himself out of the water. He reached out his hand to her, but as Randi tried to grab it, the barracuda surfaced again—directly in front of her face.

"Aaaaaaaaaagggggggghhhhhhhh!" Randi screeched hysterically as the barracuda opened its jaws, baring two dozen daggers of death. There was no way Garrett could get to her now—not with the barracuda between them.

"Swim, Randi!" Garrett cried. "Get out of his way! Head for the rocks under the pier! I can pull you up from there!"

Randi spun around fast, flailing to get away from the barracuda. Her brain was paralyzed with fear, but the adrenaline pumping through her veins kept her body moving.

She swam to the left toward the rocks, but Garrett's screams suddenly stopped her.

"Randi! Watch out!" he hollered.

Her eyes were blurred by the sting of the salt water, but she didn't need twenty-twenty vision to see what was waiting for her by the rocks. It was one of the sharks. Its massive head was out of the water, and its jaws were wide open, poised to kill.

She spun around to the right. But the second shark wasn't waiting at all. It was swimming right for her!

"Noooooooooo!"

Randi heard Garrett's cries. But it was no use. She was already looking into the enormous mouth of the murderous shark. In a second, its viselike jaws would be closing down around her as its razor-sharp teeth pierced her flesh.

There was no point in even trying to turn and swim the other way now, because shark number one was closing in behind her. The mean little barracuda was circling them both, making sure Randi stayed put.

Randi was just about to close her eyes so she wouldn't have to watch the horrible creatures attack, when the shark to her right flew out of the water sideways!

Randi heard a sickening *splat* as its enormous body landed on the pier. *What in the world is happening?* she wondered.

"Randi! Look!" Garrett pointed out over the lagoon at another creature who was flying through the air. Only this one wasn't a fish.

"It's Milo!" Randi cried as she watched the dolphin do a flip over her head before he dove back into the water.

"He's trying to save you!" Garrett exclaimed.

Milo hit the water behind her. He tore through it with the speed of a rocket, ramming the shark to her left with the top of his head.

The shark flew six feet in the air before it dropped back into the water and disappeared.

The only threat now was the barracuda.

"Randi! Come on!" Garrett waved her toward the rocks.

Randi started to swim.

The barracuda tried to get in front of her. But Milo blocked its path, butting it out of the way with his head. Within seconds, Randi was climbing onto the rocks, where Garrett was waiting.

"You okay?" Garrett asked.

Randi nodded her head. "I think so," she said. She was shivering from the cold water—and from fear. She could barely choke out the words.

"I don't know if that dolphin can talk," Garrett went on, "but he sure knows how to fight."

Out in the water, Milo was cackling like crazy—right in the barracuda's face. Two seconds later, the barracuda turned tail and took off. Milo swam to where Randi and Garrett stood on the rocks.

Randi took a step toward the water. "You saved my life," she said, looking into Milo's big brown eyes.

Milo made a clicking sound.

"What did he say?" Garrett asked.

"I don't know," Randi answered. "I think I have to touch him to be able to understand him in English."

"So touch him already," Garrett said.

Randi reached out and patted Milo's snout. She wanted to lean over and give him a big kiss, too, but Milo started to speak. His strange, gravelly voice sounded frantic.

"What's he saying?" Garrett asked, reacting to the *eee-eee-eee's* he heard.

But Randi ignored him. She was too busy listening to Milo in English.

"You must listen to me carefully," Milo told Randi. "The tooth of Nanuwee must never be replaced. It must be driven through his heart."

"What does that mean?" Randi asked Milo.

"What does *what* mean?" Garrett wanted to know.

But nobody got any answers. All at once, floodlights lit up the lagoon and sirens began to blare.

"You must get out of here." Milo's voice was still clear. "Or you won't live to see another day. Now run!"

With that, Milo disappeared under the water.

CHAPTER

11

"What do you two think you're doing down there?" an angry voice bellowed from the pier above.

"Who are you?" a second man hollered.

"Stay right where you are!" yet another commanded.

Randi wasn't about to obey. "Run!" She repeated Milo's order to Garrett.

As the hotel workers headed down the pier, Randi and Garrett took off in the other direction, across the rocks, down the path that led to the swimming pools. Randi figured that if they could get to a place where there were other people, they'd be safe. She felt sure there would be people out by the pools, lots of them.

Luckily, Randi was right. Even after dark, guests lounged by the pool and went swimming.

Randi and Garrett tried to lose themselves in the

crowd. And it seemed to work too. Nobody paid them any attention. They tried to act calm, as if they were just outside enjoying the beautiful, warm evening like everybody else. But they weren't like everybody else. They were soaking wet and scared half to death, looking over their shoulders, watching to see if they were being followed.

"It looks like we lost them," Garrett said as they headed around the kiddie pool toward the hotel entrance.

"Let's go up to my room," Randi suggested, hoping her parents would be there to protect them.

But when they got upstairs, they found the room empty.

"Double lock the door," she told Garrett once they were inside.

Garrett did as he was told while Randi walked around the room turning on all the lights.

"What the heck is going on in this place?" Garrett asked.

"I don't know," Randi answered. "But something tells me that this Feast of Nanuwee is big, big trouble."

"Why?" Garrett asked.

"Because Milo said something about Nanuwee's tooth."

Garrett looked at her as if she were nuts. "What about it?" he asked.

"He said that the tooth of Nanuwee must never be replaced," she told him. "Instead, it must be driven through his heart. What does that mean?"

"Beats me." Garrett shook his head hopelessly. "We don't even know who this Nanuwee guy is. And besides, he must have about twelve million teeth. They sell them on necklaces in the gift shops. And none of them looks big enough to drive through anybody's heart."

"I wish my family had never come here," Randi said sadly. She was standing in front of the sliding glass doors that led onto the balcony. Just the night before, she'd sat on that balcony with her parents talking about how beautiful the island was, how it really was like paradise. "I thought this was going to be a great vacation."

Garrett came up beside her. "Want to go sit outside?" he asked.

Randi thought about it for a second. Her room was three floors up, a good distance from the ground. Still, Randi wondered whether they'd be safer just staying put—until she remembered the surveillance room.

"Uh-oh," she suddenly gasped. "Maybe we *should* go outside. Somebody could be watching us right now!"

Garrett quickly unlatched the door and stepped out onto the balcony. Randi was right behind him.

But as they hurried outside, something strange caught Randi's eye. Without saying a word, she pointed it out to Garrett.

Down below, a hotel worker was skimming the pond in the little courtyard with a net. Only she wasn't skimming the surface, she was reaching deep down into the water. When she pulled up her net, it was full of beautifully colored fish.

69

Randi and Garrett exchanged nervous glances. The woman put her hand into her net, grabbed a fish by the tail, and ate it in two bites. As she reached for another, Randi and Garrett ducked back into the room and slid the door shut.

"Oh, man." Garrett shuddered. "This whole place is crawling with weirdos."

"Tell me about it." Randi cringed too.

"They're all like fish-eating freaks or something," Garrett kept rambling.

"Yeah, well, it's the 'or something' part that I'm worried about," Randi told him.

"You don't think they're eating more than the fish, do you?" Garrett asked. "I mean, you don't—"

Just then, Randi had a horrifying thought. "Shh." She cut Garrett off in a panic. "Somebody may be listening to us too!"

Garrett swallowed hard. "So what are we supposed to do?" he whispered.

"I don't know," Randi told him. "But there's definitely trouble in Paradise. And we'd better figure out what to do about it before it's too late."

CHAPTER

12

It was well past midnight before Randi finally gave up trying to convince her parents that their dream vacation was turning into a nightmare. She'd told them about the surveillance room and Mr. Kuda and the sharks and Milo's warning about Nanuwee, but they hadn't believed a word of her story. In fact, they were both looking forward to the Nanuwee feast, excited by the idea of showing off their new talents, torch tossing and hula dancing.

By seven A.M. the next morning, they were already up and raring to go to their classes. Randi's dad was even singing the "I'm a lama" song in the shower, over and over. The feast was just a day away. Randi hoped that Garrett had had better luck in convincing his parents that something was rotten in Paradise.

He hadn't. She could see it all over his face the second they met up in the lobby.

"My parent's think I'm nuts," he said as they headed off to stick-clapping class. "Especially since I made them stand in the closet to talk to me."

"Mine too," Randi informed him. "I even offered to show my dad the surveillance room. But he said that every hotel has a 'security system' in case there are problems. Then he scolded me for following Mr. Kuda in the first place. I'm telling you, both my parents are totally psyched for Nanuwee night."

"Yeah, I know," Garrett said. "My dad and your dad are torch-tossing partners. It's all my dad's been talking about."

"Terrific," Randi sighed.

"Maybe we should just skip this stick-clapping stuff today and figure out what to do."

"I don't think we can." Randi pointed to the hotel employees milling about the property. They were gathering up stragglers and shooing them off to their appropriate classes.

"Guess you're right," Garrett agreed. "The last thing we need to do is attract more attention to ourselves."

"For real," Randi said.

But the attention was already on them from the moment they reached the pavilion.

Mr. C. and Mr. Kuda were standing with the stick-clapping instructor, glaring at Randi and Garrett as they scrambled to pick up their sticks and take their seats. The instructor looked as if he'd been in some kind of accident. His chest was all black and blue, and his waist was wrapped in gauze and surgical tape. As he whispered something to Mr. C., Randi thought she caught both her name and Garrett's.

Luckily, the arrival of Bobby and Franny Farkle drew Mr. C.'s and Mr. Kuda's stares away from Randi and Garrett. Especially when Bobby Farkle tripped over Mr. Kuda's foot and slammed into the instructor's gut.

"Watch where you're going, you little beach ball," Mr. Kuda growled at Bobby.

"Ouch!" the instructor cried. "I think that kid just broke another one of my ribs."

"You broke your ribs?" Franny asked, tripping over her own feet.

The instructor nodded.

"How?" Franny wanted to know.

"I was attacked by a crazed dolphin," the instructor shot back, holding his side.

Randi and Garrett exchanged looks.

What crazed dolphin? Randi wondered nervously. *Milo? No way,* Randi told herself, shuddering at the thought.

"Hey," Bobby moaned as he headed for his seat. "Where's my pal Jimbo?"

"Jimbo who?" Mr. Kuda asked.

"Jimbo Traytor," Bobby answered. "My stick-clapping partner."

Mr. Kuda grinned. "Unfortunately, your little friend won't be joining us today," he informed Bobby. "He and his family checked out early."

"They did not!" Bobby insisted. "Jimbo and I were going to go on the giant tricycle boat down at the kiddie beach today. He said so last night! Me and him are buddies. No way he would leave here without saying good-bye!"

"Well, he did," Mr. Kuda announced. "He and his dad left the grounds after dinner last night. You'll just have to clap your sticks by yourself. Besides, you're a little too old and a little too big for the kiddie beach," he added.

"Forget it!" Bobby threw a tizzy fit along with his sticks. "I quit! I'm not even coming to Nanuwee night without Jimbo! And I'll go to the kiddie beach anytime I want!"

With that, Bobby stormed away from the group with Franny at his heels.

"You want me to handle these Farkle kids now?" Mr. Kuda whispered to Mr. C.

"Later," Mr. C. answered. "We'll deal with them later."

Garrett leaned over to whisper to Randi, but a deep voice cut him off.

"Miss Carson." Mr. C. called Randi's name.

"Yes," she answered nervously.

"*You* want to participate in the Feast of Nanuwee, don't you?" It sounded more like a threat than a question.

"Absolutely," Randi lied.

"Good," Mr. C. said. "Then why don't you show us just how much you've learned so far in this class."

Yikes!

"You can start by singing the Nanuwee song," he said.

For the first time all morning, Randi was grateful that her parents had been acting like a couple of Nanuwee nuts. If her father hadn't been singing the "lama" song in the shower, she never would have remembered it. But luckily, it was drilled into her head. She started to sing it with all of her heart.

"Ama lama, kooma lama, kooma lama, beast day," she belted. "Oh, no, no, not the beast day. Itchy-goomy, mela-loomy, nuwe-nama, wonder-ama. Ba, bam, boo."

Garrett's jaw dropped as Mr. C.'s pale lips turned up into a creepy grin. "Wonderful," Mr. C. told her. "I expect that you'll keep up the good work."

Randi nodded, heaving a sigh of relief.

"I'm sure that I don't have to remind you to obey the rules of this property," he added.

"No, sir," Randi said.

"Good," Mr. C. responded. "Now, let's see how the rest of the group is coming along."

Without Bobby, Franny, and Jimbo, the rest of the group was actually coming along pretty well. Every stick was clacking in rhythm, and every voice was singing in tune.

Mr. C. applauded the effort. "You're doing much better today. The great spirit of Nanuwee will be pleased."

"In more ways than one way," Mr. Kuda added.

"That's right." Mr. C. laughed. "Tomorrow night, when all the groups come together, our guests will see just how pleased Nanuwee will be."

With that, Mr. C. and Mr. Kuda headed over to check on the torch-tossing class while the instructor made the stick clappers take it from the top again. An hour and a half later, the group was dismissed.

There was no question as to what Randi wanted to do next. She wanted to get to Milo to ask him about Nanuwee and his tooth, not to mention the rest of the weirdness that was going on around them.

But Garrett was hungry. He begged her to go to the restaurant with him to get something to eat first, since they'd both skipped breakfast.

Randi agreed, as long as they ate fast.

The problem was, everyone else at the resort seemed to have skipped breakfast too. The line for the buffet table was wrapped around the restaurant like a snake.

Randi wasn't about to wait. "Let's just get a hot dog down at the snack bar," she told Garrett. "We can eat it on the way over to the dolphin lagoon."

"Okay," Garrett agreed, stepping out of line. "If we go out the back doors near the kitchen, it's a shorter walk to the beach."

"Fine by me," Randi said, zigzagging behind Garrett to make their way through the hungry crowd.

"Come on," Garrett urged as he pushed open the doors to the outside. "I'll race you."

Randi was about to take Garrett up on his challenge when something on the ground outside the door caught her eye.

"Garrett, look," she said, pointing to the multicolored Hawaiian-flowered bow tie lying by his foot. "It's Mr. Traytor's bow tie, the one he was wearing at dinner last night."

"Maybe it fell off," Garrett suggested, bending down to pick it up.

"I doubt it," Randi said. "Didn't you see how tight he wears his bow ties? They practically strangle him. There's no way it would just fall off."

"Well, maybe he took it off," Garrett responded hopefully.

Randi rolled her eyes. "Yeah, right. He was swimming in one yesterday," she told him. "He probably even wears bow ties to bed."

"So what are you saying?" Garrett asked.

Randi couldn't even believe what she was thinking—until something else caught her eye. "What's that?" she said, pointing to the giant Dumpster on the side of the building.

"The Dumpster the restaurant uses," Garrett answered.

"I know that," Randi told him. "I mean what's that sticking out of it?"

"It looks like luggage," Garrett said, taking a step toward it. "That's weird. Why would anyone put their luggage in a Dumpster?"

Randi didn't reply. She just stood there staring at the tag that was dangling from the handle of one of the bags. Written in perfect penmanship were the names "B. A. Traytor and Jimbo."

CHAPTER 13

"Bobby Farkle was right!" Randi exclaimed in horror. "Jimbo and his dad didn't check out. They couldn't have. Their luggage is still here. And so are all their clothes." She pulled a pair of Jimbo's shorts from one of the bags.

"This isn't good," Garrett said, shaking his head.

"Come on," Randi urged, tugging Garrett's arm. "We have to get to Milo."

Randi and Garrett didn't bother to stop at the snack bar. Instead, they raced straight to the rope bridge and headed for the pier.

"Uh-oh," Garrett said, pointing ahead. "I don't think we're going to be able to get there today."

A huge red sign was chained across the entrance to the pier. It read No More Dolphin Encounters in big, block letters, followed by the words Keep Out!

"They probably don't want anyone near there because of what happened last night," Garrett said.

"Tough," Randi declared. She bent down and ducked under the chain and onto the pier. "You coming?" she asked, turning back to Garrett.

"I'm not so sure this is such a good idea anymore," Garrett told her. "I mean, what if we get attacked again?"

Randi didn't even want to think about that. "Look," she said, "if we don't find Milo, we're never going to figure out what's going on around here. Besides, Milo said the danger was *all* around us. Not just in the water."

"You swear you can hear this fish talk?" Garrett asked.

"No," Randi huffed. "I'm making it up. Of course I hear him talk! I wouldn't be risking my life if I didn't."

Garrett took a deep breath and finally stepped under the chain. "Do me a favor," he said. "When you tap the water this time, stand on the rocks and then back way, way up, until we're sure we recognize the fin. Okay?"

"Deal," Randi agreed.

But there was no way either one of them was even going to get close to the rocks. And there was no way Randi was going to stick her hand in those waters. They were only halfway down the pier when three dozen fins surfaced.

Within seconds, one shark after another leaped from the water, nipping the air as if he was searching for flesh.

One thing was clear. If Milo was in those waters, there was no way he was alive. Fighting a couple of sharks was one thing, but fighting an army was another.

Terror pierced Randi's heart like a shark's tooth. She could barely breathe as she looked out into the jaws of death. Suddenly, her head started to spin.

Down in the churning water below her was Barry Kuda's name tag.

CHAPTER

14

Randi and Garrett stood staring down at the name tag as it swirled in the shark-infested water.

Garrett gulped. "Looks like something bad might have happened to Mr. Kuda," he said.

"Might have?" Randi asked. It was pretty clear to her that Mr. Kuda had ended up as shark food. This place was getting more horrifying by the minute.

"Let's get out of here," Garrett suggested.

As they turned to go, Randi saw that they were being watched. But it was *who* was watching them that made Randi gasp in surprise.

Mr. Kuda was standing beside Mr. C. on the pathway above them. The two men stared down at Randi and Garrett but didn't say a word.

"Hi," Randi said, smiling nervously.

"Yeah, hi," Garrett echoed.

They got no answer from the men, who continued to stand motionless, their arms crossed in front of them, looking as though they'd just caught Randi and Garrett committing a crime.

"We just came down here for the Dolphin Encounter," Randi said nervously.

Mr. C. and Mr. Kuda kept right on glaring at them.

"I guess there isn't a Dolphin Encounter today," Garrett added. "So we'll just do something else instead." He grabbed Randi's arm and started leading her away.

"See you later," she called over her shoulder to Mr. C. and Mr. Kuda, whose eyes were practically burning holes through her and Garrett.

"Whatever's going on around here," Garrett whispered to Randi as they picked up their pace, "those two are in on it."

"No," Randi disagreed. "Those two are in *charge* of it. And I'm afraid they know that we're on to them." Randi glanced back to see the two men following them at a distance.

"On to them?" Garrett shook his head. "We don't have a clue as to what's really going on around here."

They started across the rope bridge toward the kiddie beach. Randi watched as shark fins traced circles in the water beneath them.

"We know one thing," she told Garrett. "There's danger all around."

A shrill scream from up ahead punctuated Randi's point.

"What was that?" Garrett cried as the two of them took off running toward the sound.

"Help!" a woman's voice shrieked. "Help! My boy is missing!"

The cries were coming from the kiddie beach, where a crowd had already begun to gather.

At the center of the crowd were three of the Farkles.

"My Bobby is missing," Mrs. Farkle wailed. "Something terrible has happened to him. I just know it."

As Randi and Garrett approached the group of people who had surrounded the Farkles, Randi scanned the beach for any sign of Bobby. But there was none—just his purple flip-flops, the neon sunblock, and the beach bag full of munchies sitting on Bobby's Superman towel in the sand.

"Where was your son when you last saw him?" a woman asked, putting her arm around Mrs. Farkle.

But Mrs. Farkle was too busy sobbing to answer.

"He was out there," Franny answered for her mother, pointing toward the water. "He was riding that giant water tricycle."

But he wasn't riding it anymore. The giant water tricycle was tipped over on its side.

Mrs. Farkle was right. Something was wrong. Randi knew it. She shook her head hopelessly as she watched the water tricycle bobbing in the water, Bobby-less.

CHAPTER 15

Mr. C. and Mr. Kuda joined the crowd on the kiddie beach.

"What seems to be the problem?" Mr. C. asked Mrs. Farkle in a voice full of concern.

Randi and Garrett tried to blend in with the rest of the crowd as they listened.

"My Bobby is missing," Mrs. Farkle cried. "We can't find him anywhere."

Mr. C. turned to Mr. Kuda. Randi thought that for a second, the expression on Mr. C.'s face looked awfully angry.

Then Mr. C. and Mr. Kuda whispered to each other for a few moments. When Mr. C. turned his attention back to Mrs. Farkle, he had a tight-lipped smile plastered on his face.

"Just humor me, okay?" Randi said to him.

Garrett shrugged and followed Randi down the long hallway toward the reception area, where the elevators were. Randi pushed the button to go up and stood waiting, and worrying, and wondering what they would find once they got to the Farkles' room.

But Garrett was busy looking around.

"I've got an idea," he said just as the elevator arrived.

There was no one on it. In fact, there was no one anywhere to be seen.

"Let's check the computers," Garrett suggested, nodding toward the empty reservations desk.

Randi let the elevator doors close in front of her. "Good thinking," she told Garrett.

Garrett was already moving toward the computers. Randi rushed to catch up.

"Let's see what we can find out," Garrett said as he went around the back of the desk.

Randi positioned herself in front, keeping a lookout to make sure they didn't get caught.

Garrett started tapping away at the machine.

"You must really know what you're doing," Randi commented.

"Yeah." Garrett smiled proudly. "I'm pretty good with these things." His smile disappeared. "Uh-oh," he said, staring at the monitor.

"What's wrong?" Randi asked, straining to peek over the desk.

"You're not going to believe this," Garrett told her.

His eyes were riveted to the computer screen.

Randi went around the desk to have a look for herself.

Garrett had accessed the guest list for the hotel. All of the names were up on the screen. But two names in particular caught Randi's eye—Farkle and Traytor.

Randi gasped as she read what had been typed in bold letters next to their names: EATEN.

CHAPTER 16

Randi couldn't believe her eyes as she stared at the screen in front of her. "No wonder the Traytors' luggage was in the Dumpster," she said. "They didn't go home! They were eaten! Right along with the Farkles!"

Garrett's face had turned as white as the underbelly of a shark. "Oh, man! That Kuda guy wasn't kidding when he said Jimbo and his dad had 'checked out'!"

Suddenly Garrett grabbed Randi's arm and pulled her to the floor behind the counter. "Get down," he said. "The manager's coming."

"We have to get out of here!" Randi whispered, crouching down beside him.

As the front desk manager rounded the counter to their right, Randi and Garrett scrambled to their left. The second they were out of view, they ran for the door.

"Now what?" Randi sighed as they hit the outdoors. "No way our parents are going to believe that the Farkles and the Traytors were eaten. And without Milo, we're never going to be able to find out what's really going on around here."

"Maybe we can," Garrett said. "Maybe if we sneak back into the control room under the shark lagoon, we can spy on Mr. C. and Mr. Kuda," he suggested. "Maybe they'll say something or do something that will give us a clue."

"Good thinking!" Randi exclaimed as the two of them took off running.

Luckily, the tunnel under the shark lagoon was deserted. So was the control room.

"Look for a button that says 'Mr. C.'s office,'" Randi told Garrett as they stood over the keyboard. Above them, all the monitors were running. Randi could even see her parents out by the pool with Garrett's parents, practicing the hula.

"There's no button for Mr. C.'s office," Garrett informed her.

"What about Mr. Kuda's office?" Randi asked.

"Nope," Garrett replied. "Just the hotel rooms and the rest of the resort."

"Wait a minute," Randi said. "Maybe if you try typing in the words 'Mr. C.'s office,' it'll come up."

"Good idea," Garrett agreed. He started typing in the letters. The moment he finished, every monitor in the room started to flash. Some even started to beep because the sound knobs were turned up. But across *every* screen ran the words WARNING! ENTER YOUR FIN NUMBER NOW!

"Do something!" Randi shrieked, twisting down the sound knobs before the beeping boxes attracted attention.

"I don't have a fin number!" Garrett yelped. "I don't even know what that is!"

"Push the escape key," Randi told him. "That's what I always do when I mess up on my computer. Maybe that'll fix it."

Garrett hit the escape key fast. A moment later, the monitors above them were showing exactly what they had shown before, locations on the property.

"Whew," Garrett sighed. "That was a close call."

"Try Mr. Kuda's office," Randi said. "Maybe that one will work."

Garrett typed in the command, but again, the screens flashed the warning ENTER YOUR FIN NUMBER NOW!

"Looks like they don't want anybody spying on *them*," Garrett declared, hitting the escape key again.

Just then Randi's eye caught an image on the monitor to her left. "Garrett," she said, pointing up to it, "look. We don't need to see into Mr. C.'s office. Because there he is! And Mr. Kuda is with him."

"So is our stick-clapping instructor," Garrett added. "It looks like they're right outside on the rocks above the shark lagoon."

Randi quickly turned up the sound knob. Immediately, Mr. C.'s voice boomed out of the speaker and echoed throughout the control room. He was screaming at Mr. Kuda.

"The Traytors were one thing," Mr. C. shouted. "But I gave you strict orders to keep the Farkles alive! We need every *body* we can get for the Feast of Nanuwee! Between the Farkles and the Traytors, we're already down six!"

"It wasn't my fault, boss," Mr. Kuda shot back. "It was this stupid hammerhead here!" He pointed to their stick-clapping instructor. "He's the one who didn't follow orders. He was supposed to drag that Farkle kid back to class, not out to the shark lagoon."

Randi and Garrett exchanged horrified looks.

Up on the monitor, Mr. C. grabbed the instructor by the throat. "Because of you, I had to swallow the rest of those Farkle freaks. I've been sick to my stomach all day!"

"I'm telling you, Mr. C.," the instructor pleaded, "I did you a favor by getting rid of that kid. There's no way he would have helped raise Nanuwee. He couldn't even clap his own sticks together, much less clap with the rest of the group!"

"Save your breath," Mr. C. growled. "You're going to need it."

With that, Mr. C. pushed the instructor off the rocks—into the shark lagoon.

Randi and Garrett watched in stunned silence as the instructor changed from a man into a hammerhead shark under the water.

Mr. C. and Mr. Kuda dove into the lagoon after him.

The instant they hit the water, they changed too.

Mr. Kuda turned into a slimy silver barracuda. And Mr. C. . . . He became a great white shark—bigger than any shark Randi had ever seen.

The two monsters moved through the water like guided missiles, straight for the hammerhead.

Within seconds, the great white ripped the hammerhead in two, devouring the top half of its body in one quick bite. Meanwhile, the barracuda chowed down on its tail.

"I can't believe this is happening!" Garrett stared in horror at the sight.

Randi turned her head, unable to watch any more.

"It's over," Garrett said finally.

Randi turned back to the monitor to see the shark and the barracuda swim out of view.

There was nothing left of the hammerhead—just as there was nothing left of the Farkles and the Traytors.

The blood flowing through Randi's veins felt ice cold. "We've got to get out of here," she managed to say to Garrett. She knew that if anyone caught them in that room, there would be nothing left of them either.

CHAPTER 17

Randi ran to the door of the control room and threw it open. But she stopped short.

There were voices echoing inside the tunnel, voices she recognized.

She held Garrett back, and the two of them stood listening.

"I hate hammerhead meat," Mr. C. was complaining. "It's chewy and tough. And totally tasteless," he added. "It's already starting to repeat on me, just like those foul-tasting Farkles."

"Tell me about it," Mr. Kuda chimed in. "Even that Jimbo kid and his pathetic little dad were more succulent than that stick-clapping fool."

Mr. C. laughed. "It's a shame we can't sink our teeth into some of the more tender guests for dessert."

"Don't worry about it," Mr. Kuda told him. "After the Feast of Nanuwee, we'll be able to sink our teeth into anything we want. And we won't have to go back into the water to do it."

Randi shot Garrett a look.

"That's what I'm living for, Barry," Mr. C. said.

Suddenly, Randi realized that the voices were getting closer. Mr. C. and Mr. Kuda were headed toward the control room.

She pushed Garrett back and closed the door as quietly as she could. "We've got to hide!"

"Where?" Garrett asked hopelessly as his eyes scanned the room. Then he found an answer to his own question. "Maybe we can get into this thing," he suggested, running toward the mysterious submarinelike hatch in the wall.

Randi raced to his side. But neither of them could get the steel wheel to budge.

"It's no use," Randi cried. "We've got to get out of here!"

"Unless you and I can morph into mice," Garrett shot back, "there's no way we're going to get past those two fin-backed freaks—at least not alive!"

Randi looked up at the monitor, hoping to spot an escape route. But Mr. C. and Mr. Kuda had them trapped. They were headed straight for the door. "They're coming!" Randi shrieked.

Garrett ran around the room, frantically searching for cover. As the doorknob started to turn, Randi plastered herself behind the door, like a sheet of wallpaper.

Garrett quickly did the same.

In front of them, the door opened a crack.

"What in the name of Nanuwee is this door doing unlocked?" Mr. C. growled. "How many times have I told you to keep this room secure, Barry?"

"I guess I forgot to lock it last night," Mr. Kuda answered.

"How could you be so stupid?" Mr. C. bellowed.

"I wasn't stupid, boss," Mr. Kuda said defensively. "I was just in a hurry. I'd been out of the water for more than twelve hours and I needed to get to the decompression tank fast. If I had stopped to lock the door, I would be dead."

"Well, don't let it happen again," Mr. C. barked. Then he pushed the door open as far as it would go.

Randi held her breath as the doorknob hit her right in the gut. She was sure that Mr. C. was going to spot them and that she and Garrett were about to end up as the tender dessert Mr. C. had wanted.

But Mr. C. didn't step into the room. Instead, he eyed the room quickly, turned the lock on the knob, and pulled the door shut again.

Randi and Garrett stood frozen.

Outside, Mr. C. and Mr. Kuda were still talking. Randi could hear them through the door and see them on the monitor.

"Have you sent the nurse sharks over to the Sacred Pagoda yet?" Mr. C. asked.

Mr. Kuda nodded. "They're sterilizing the tooth of Nanuwee as we speak."

"Good," Mr. C. said. "Let's go see that they're preparing it properly."

Randi watched the screen as Mr. C. and Mr. Kuda moved toward the exit. The moment she felt safe, she let out a gasp. "Did you hear what they said?"

"You mean about the tooth?" Garrett asked, doubling over to catch his breath.

Randi nodded. "Milo was right. There really is a tooth of Nanuwee. It's in their Sacred Pagoda."

"Where the heck is that?" Garrett wondered.

"I don't know," Randi said, heading for the keyboard. She wasn't really expecting to see a button that said "Sacred Pagoda," but she searched the keyboard anyway. This time, when she started to type in the words, she had a pretty good idea what would happen.

WARNING! The bright red letters flashed on the screens. ENTER YOUR FIN NUMBER NOW!

"It's no use," Garrett said. "There's no way we're going to be able to see anything around this place that they don't want us to see."

"Oh, yes, there is," Randi told him, suddenly getting an idea.

Garrett's eyes narrowed.

"Mr. C. and Mr. Kuda are headed for the Sacred Pagoda, right?" Randy asked.

"So?" Garrett said.

"Soooooo," Randi went on, "while they're over there,

we can break into Mr. C.'s office. I guarantee you, there's plenty of information in there."

"No way," Garrett declared, shaking his head. "It's too dangerous. Do you know what will happen to us if we get caught?"

Randi didn't even want to think about that. "It's a chance we're going to have to take."

CHAPTER 18

Mr. C.'s office was large and impressive, and surprisingly easy to sneak into.

"*Everybody* must be at the Sacred Pagoda," Garrett said as he quietly closed the door behind them.

Randi's eyes darted about the room, looking for anything that would give her a clue. But Mr. C.'s office looked just like the typical office of a very powerful man.

But as Garrett and Randi had found out, Mr. C. was not a man.

"Look at this," Garrett exclaimed, pointing to a portrait on the wall behind Mr. C.'s desk.

"It's a picture of a shark," Randi said, not getting Garrett's point at first.

"Yes," Garrett responded a little impatiently. "But look at the plaque underneath the picture."

Randi read it out loud. "Carcharodon Carcharias." The moment she said it, her heart skipped a beat. "Isn't that Mr. C.'s full name?"

"Yeah," Garrett answered. "And this is a self-portrait! Look."

Randi studied the picture. It was definitely Mr. C.—in his fish form.

"Check it out," Garrett said, pointing to the words beneath the plaque. "*Carcharodon carcharias* is the scientific name for the great white shark." Garrett swallowed hard. "You don't think that *all* the people who work at this hotel are sharks, do you?"

Randi nodded. "Except for Mr. Kuda. Mr. Barry-Kuda!"

"Oh, man." Garrett cringed. "Where did all these fish-morphing freaks come from? And what the heck are they doing running a resort in the Caribbean?"

The answer was right in front of their eyes.

Garrett spotted it first. "Look at this," he cried, heading for an enormous table in the corner of the room.

"What is that supposed to be?" Randi asked as she followed.

Set up on the table was a model of a city. It looked like an ancient city with large, open squares, domed buildings, and marble pillars.

"'Zoomorphia.'" Garrett read the name of the city from the grand archway at its entrance.

As Garrett stood studying the model, Randi noticed a piece of rolled parchment on the table. She picked it up, unrolled it, and silently scanned the words that were written on it.

"This must be a design for a new addition they're planning to build," Garrett said finally.

"No," Randi told him, looking up from her reading. "Zoomorphia is not a *new* addition they're planning to build. Zoomorphia is a sunken city they're planning to raise from the bottom of the ocean."

"How are they going to do that?" Garrett asked.

"That's what the Feast of Nanuwee is all about," Randi explained.

Garrett looked over Randi's shoulder as she began to read aloud from the parchment. "'The great spirit Nanuwee can be summoned only by the sound of human voices, hundreds strong, singing his praises.'"

"Then that's why Carcharodon Carcharias built this resort—to attract hundreds of humans to call up Nanuwee," Garrett said.

"Right," Randi agreed, reading ahead. "'Only Nanuwee can raise up the city of Zoomorphia.'"

"Is that such a bad thing?" Garrett asked.

"It's a really bad thing," Randi said as she continued to read. "'When Zoomorphia rises from the sea, the earth will suffer tidal waves, earthquakes, and other catastrophes that will cover all the land with ocean waters. Zoomorphia will be the only city on earth.'"

"That's pretty bad," Garrett gulped.

"And that's not even the worst of it," Randi continued. "Before Nanuwee raises Zoomorphia, he must be offered a feast, a *human* feast."

"What?" Garrett shrieked.

"That's why we're here." Randi had it all figured out. "That's why every family on this island got a free vacation! *We're* the feast of Nanuwee!"

CHAPTER 19

"We've got to get out of here," Randi insisted to her mother and father. "We've got to get *everyone* out of here before the Feast of Nanuwee!"

But the two of them just sat shaking their heads, refusing to listen.

"Randi," Mrs. Carson reprimanded her, "I've had just about all I'm going to take of this nonsense."

"I agree," Mrs. Brown said, glaring at Garrett.

The two families were sitting at a table by the pool, having breakfast together.

Randi and Garrett had tried everything they could think of to convince their parents to leave the island before the Feast of Nanuwee that night. They had even admitted to sneaking into Mr. C.'s office. But nothing they said changed their parents' minds.

"Your behavior has been inexcusable," Mr. Brown added.

"I simply can't believe that you would break into someone's private office," Mr. Carson said, shaking his head sadly at his daughter.

"But you're not listening to what we found in there," Randi protested.

"I'm sure there's a logical explanation for everything you saw," Mrs. Carson declared. "That's not the point."

"The point is," Mrs. Brown went on, "what the two of you did was wrong."

"I have half a mind to march you down to Mr. C.'s office right now so that you can apologize to him personally," Mr. Brown said.

"No!" Garrett gasped. "Don't do that. He'll eat me!"

All four parents let out one giant sigh in unison.

"I give up," Mrs. Carson said, throwing her hands in the air.

"Why don't the two of you take a walk," Mr. Carson suggested to Randi and Garrett. "Give us some time to discuss what we should do about this situation."

Randi got up from the table, knowing that if she said another word, she and Garrett would only be in bigger trouble with their parents. They couldn't risk being grounded and possibly being separated from each other. They needed each other. And their parents, and every other guest on that island, needed them too, even though nobody understood that. They had to find a way to prevent the Feast of Nanuwee.

"What now?" Garrett said once they were out of earshot of their parents.

Randi didn't answer. She didn't have an answer.

The two of them walked silently down the path that led onto the beach. All around them people were having fun, unaware that this might be the last day they ever saw.

When Randi and Garrett reached the end of the path, they saw a group of hotel employees working down on the beach, preparing for the feast. They were setting out torches and flowers and tents.

Randi and Garrett stopped to watch. Maybe they would see or hear something that would help them come up with a plan.

"What's that?" Garrett asked Randi. He pointed to an object at the center of the activity. It was covered with a tarp and was sitting on top of an enormous platform on wheels. It took two dozen men to push the platform forward.

"I don't know." Randi shrugged. "Maybe it's a statue of Nanuwee."

"I'll bet that's exactly what it is," Garrett said.

But they were wrong.

One of the workers began pulling away the tarp. "Behold," he said as the others stopped to watch. "The tooth of Nanuwee!"

Randi and Garrett both gasped at the sight.

The tooth of Nanuwee was as big as a sailboat.

"That is one scary-looking tooth," Garrett said.

"Yeah," Randi agreed. "And if that's Nanuwee's tooth, I really don't think we want to meet Nanuwee."

CHAPTER 20

Luckily, Randi and Garrett managed to convince their parents to put off punishing them until after they'd gotten home. Their parents had threatened to confine them in their separate rooms. But since it was their last day at the resort, and since Randi and Garrett admitted that what they had done was wrong, their parents relented.

They spent the whole day trying to figure out a way to stop Nanuwee night from coming.

Randi wished she could go to Milo for advice. But Milo was gone, probably eaten by sharks.

Randi and Garrett were on their own. The situation seemed hopeless. The only plan the two of them could come up with was impossible to accomplish.

There was no way they could steal the tooth of

Nanuwee, not when two dozen fish-freaks were guarding it. And even if they managed to get to the tooth, there was no way to move the thing—and no place to hide it.

As the sun set into the sea and darkness surrounded the island, Randi and Garrett had no choice but to follow their parents down to the beach, where the Feast of Nanuwee was about to begin.

"Welcome." Mr. C. greeted the crowd as soon as every guest was present and accounted for. He was standing at the foot of Nanuwee's tooth, smiling like the shark he was.

Mr. Kuda was beside him, baring *his* jaw full of spears.

"We're so pleased to have you with us this evening," Mr. C. continued. "Aren't we, Barry?"

"Not nearly as pleased as we will be when we get this show on the road," Barry Kuda shot back.

"I'll bet," Garrett whispered to Randi. They were sitting with the rest of the stick clappers, under the stick-clapping tent. They'd been herded to their "appropriate seats" the moment they'd hit the beach.

Randi looked toward her mother. She was sitting under the hula tent, right near the shell-blowing bunch. But she was so busy fussing with her hula skirt and giggling with Garrett's mom, she didn't see the fear in Randi's eyes. In fact, the two moms were acting like a couple of school-girls about to put on their first play.

Little did they know, it would also be their last.

Randi started to shiver. She wanted to run to her dad. She could see him standing with the other men, holding his torch proudly. And while he looked like a human matchstick, Randi knew that by the time the night was through, he'd be nothing more than fish fondue.

"We have to stop this," she whispered to Garrett in a panic. "We have to do something!"

"Silence," the new stick-clapping instructor ordered. "Mr. C. is talking."

Randi's eyes quickly moved back to the tooth of Nanuwee. Mr. C. and Mr. Kuda were still standing beneath it, leering at the crowd.

"As you know," Mr. C. went on, "the Feast of Nanuwee is a very special occasion for us here at Paradise. And you are a very special part of it. In fact," the shark in the white suit snickered, "without you, there wouldn't even be a feast. Isn't that right, Barry?"

Barry Kuda nodded. "Absolutely, boss." He laughed too.

Randi shot Garrett a look.

"Therefore," Mr. C. continued, "it is important that you all sing your hearts out while you perform your tasks perfectly. We have only one chance to get this right. And it will all be over with before you know it."

That was exactly what Randi was afraid of.

"Let the ceremony begin!" Mr. Kuda ordered.

With that, they all rose from their seats as the instructors counted down to show time.

"On three," the stick-clapping creep began. "One . . ."

"Don't sing," Randi told Garrett under her breath. "Just mouth the words so it looks like you're singing."

"Two . . ."

"And don't really clap your sticks together either," she said. "Maybe if the two of us stay silent, nothing will happen."

"Three!"

Around them, the sticks clacked. The drums beat. The shells blew. Fireballs tore through the air as torch tossers passed their batons. Belly buttons wiggled in hula skirts, and streamers danced through the sky.

Randi's eyes darted about the beach nervously, watching for the arrival of Nanuwee.

"Nothing's happening," Randi whispered to Garrett, feeling a little relieved.

"Maybe nothing will," Garrett whispered back. "Maybe you're right. Maybe if we don't join in the chant, Nanuwee won't come."

But the "I'm a lama" song had just begun.

Every voice, except for two, rose up in harmony. And as Nanuwee's praises were sung, something strange started to happen. Something that Randi and Garrett had never anticipated.

At first, Randi thought it was just her imagination. But she really was starting to feel woozy. Her head was getting light and her eyes felt out of focus. Her limbs began to tingle as if they were falling asleep. While the voices around her grew louder, they sounded farther away.

"I don't know about you," Garrett mumbled, as if there were a wad of cotton in his mouth, "but all of a sudden, I don't feel so well."

"I feel weird too," Randi told him. "This Nanuwee song is making me sick."

Randi struggled to see Mr. C. and Mr. Kuda through her blurred vision. They were still near the tooth of Nanuwee, grinning from ear to ear. Dozens of workers were with them, tying huge ropes around the tooth.

Just then, the "I'm a lama" song ended with a big "Ba, bam, boo."

But no one applauded. And nobody moved.

Randi tried to focus on the rest of the guests. Through the haze she could see that none of them was even smiling. In fact, they had no expressions at all. Every face in the crowd was blank, and every eye vacant.

Randi's heart dropped to the pit of her stomach. *No wonder the Nanuwee song was so important!* Randi realized. The song had put everyone in a trance—everyone but her and Garrett. It was a good thing they hadn't joined in.

There was nothing but stillness and silence . . . until Mr. C. shouted, "It's time to replace the tooth of Nanuwee!"

Immediately, two dozen shark people began wheeling the tooth of Nanuwee down to the edge of the sea. The moment they reached the wet sand, they came to a stop. And Mr. C. gave the rest of his orders.

"Now put the women at the head of the line, towing the ropes, and the men in the back to push. The children we'll save until the end. Move them all out!" he commanded. "The moment Nanuwee rises, we must be ready."

Two seconds later, the Nanuwee instructors were lining up their groups.

Randi almost panicked when she saw the hula instructor dragging her mom toward the water. She moved along in a daze, staring ahead like a zombie.

So did all the other women.

"Oh, my gosh," Randi whispered, grabbing Garrett's arm. "They don't even know what's happening!"

"What are we going to do?" Garrett asked as he watched his own mom and dad being led to the tooth of Nanuwee.

But Randi didn't answer. Because suddenly her attention was drawn to something so horrifying, she had to fight the urge to scream.

Rising up from the water near the horizon were two hundred fins. Within seconds, they were moving toward the tooth of Nanuwee with greater speed than Carcharodon Carcharias himself.

CHAPTER

21

"Sharks!" Randi screamed, staring out at the water.

"Oh, man," Garrett cried. "Our parents are headed straight for the ocean."

Randi shouted at the rest of the kids standing around them. "Wake up, you morons!" She shook the freckle-faced kid beside her. "Our parents are about to get eaten by sharks!"

But none of the stick-clapping clowns even batted an eye. They just kept clapping their sticks together as they lined up behind the adults to walk out into the sea.

"Come on," Randi said as she grabbed Garrett's arm and ran for the water.

"What are you going to do?" Garrett yelped.

"I'm going to drag my mom and dad out of there before they get ripped to shreds," Randi answered. "And if I were you, I'd do the same!"

As Randi hit the surf, she saw her dad. He was trudging along behind the tooth of Nanuwee, pushing the platform forward. But Randi didn't stop running. She raced past her dad and headed straight for her mom. Her dad was only in up to his knees, but her mom was already in way past her waist. She was marching three feet in front of the tooth, pulling one of the ropes.

"Mom!" Randi shouted as she tugged at her mother's arm. "You have to get out of this water!"

Her mother didn't even look at her.

"Please, Mom!" Randi begged. "You've got to snap out of it!"

Less than a hundred feet in front of her, the fins began to close in.

Randi screamed hysterically. She tried to pull her mom away from the rope by her waist, then her legs, then her hair. But her mother wouldn't stop walking. Randi even bit her mother's hand, but her mother was holding the rope so tightly, it was as if her fingers were glued to the twine.

"Randi!" Garrett called.

Randi spun around to see Garrett standing behind the platform, yanking on his dad. Farther back on the beach, Mr. C. and Mr. Kuda stood watching. Their lips were twisted in evil smiles.

"I can't get my dad to stop," Garrett cried. "He won't even look at me! And neither will my mom!"

"I know!" Randi shouted back. "Neither will mine!"

Just then, Garrett let out a scream that rattled the tooth

of Nanuwee. He was staring out at the water past Randi. And the look on his face told Randi all she needed to know even before she turned back around.

There, lined up in front of the tooth of Nanuwee, were hundreds of sharks in two dozen rows.

Randi was too terrified to breathe. She was standing face-to-fin with Carcharodon's army of death!

Then one of the creatures lifted its head and swam a foot closer.

Randi blinked hard as she stared into the creature's brown eyes. These weren't the eyes of a shark! And they weren't the eyes of a fish either. They were the eyes of a dolphin.

"Milo!" she shrieked. "You're alive!"

"Eeeeee-eeee-eeee!" Milo answered in a frantic cackle. The army behind him surfaced as well. It wasn't an army of sharks; it was an army of dolphins.

Randi quickly reached out to touch Milo's snout. As soon as she did, Milo began to speak in a human voice.

"Nanuwee is rising," Milo told her. "There isn't much time."

Just then, Mr. Kuda's voice tore through the air. "The dolphins have arrived!" he shouted. "The traitorous dolphins are here!"

Randi spun around to see Mr. Kuda and Mr. C. storming down the beach.

"Get in there and rip off their fins," Mr. C. raged at Mr. Kuda as he stopped at the edge of the water.

"Impossible," Barry Kuda snapped. "Until Nanuwee

rises, that water will fry us like trout. You know the rules. On Nanuwee night, no other shark is allowed in the water until Nanuwee accepts his feast."

"But you're a barracuda!" Mr. C. bit back.

"Let me tell you something, boss," Barry Kuda huffed. "Even if I were a giant white whale I wouldn't get in that water. Not until Nanuwee gives the okay. No way I'm taking any chances."

Randi couldn't believe her ears. Maybe everyone really was safer in the water now that all the sharks were up on land.

"Randi!" Milo said suddenly. "Forget about those Zoomorphians and listen to me!"

Randi looked back at Milo. "Is that what they're called? Zoomorphians?"

"Yes, yes," Milo answered. "But we haven't got time for a history lesson right now. You must do as I say. And you must do it quickly."

Suddenly, the waters around them turned rough. Giant waves rose in the distance and rolled to the shore like thunder. Up on the beach, the wind began blowing so hard, palm trees were bending and snapping like twigs.

"What's going on?" Garrett screamed to Randi.

But Randi didn't answer. Because Mr. C. did.

"Nanuwee!" he exclaimed. "Nanuwee is coming!"

"You see, boss?" Mr. Kuda chimed in. "We don't have to worry about those stupid dolphins. Nanuwee will annihilate 'em."

Just then, every dolphin behind Milo started to move.

But they weren't swimming away. They were swimming toward the people holding the ropes.

Randi watched as the dolphins used the tips of their snouts to bump the adults out of the way and into the surf, leaving them flailing in the water, unable to hold on to the ropes.

"What are they doing?" Randi shrieked.

Milo didn't answer. Instead, he gave her an order. "Climb up on the tooth of Nanuwee," he said. "Now. Or prepare to die."

Randi's heart started pumping so hard, she could barely breath. *Maybe Milo isn't a nice dolphin! Maybe he's some kind of Zoomorphian too! Maybe all the creatures around this place are trying to kill us!*

"Get on the tooth!" Milo insisted. "It must be delivered to Nanuwee by a human!"

Randi knew that she had no choice but to obey. The water out by the horizon was starting to spin like a whirlpool. The dolphins were getting as antsy as sharks, chattering frantically.

With all the courage she could muster, Randi hoisted herself out of the water and onto the platform. Then she climbed onto the giant, speared tooth and straddled it as though it were a horse.

The moment she did, the tooth of Nanuwee shot forward. Two hundred dolphins were propelling it out to sea by the ropes that were now wrapped around their snouts.

"Randi!" Garrett's voice cried out behind her.

"*Noooooooooo!* Get off that tooth! It's too dangerous!"

But Randi didn't turn around. She was too busy hanging on for dear life.

The great Nanuwee started to rise. The creature was as big as a whale, with eyes that glowed red like two volcanos about to erupt.

Randi screamed as the dolphins sped forward, pulling her and Nanuwee's tooth toward the creature's huge face.

Randi was headed straight for Nanuwee's jaws, which opened as wide as a train tunnel.

CHAPTER 22

Randi was sure she was about to become the first human sacrifice to Nanuwee.

What if Milo and the other dolphins are all in on Mr. C.'s plan? she thought. What if she'd just fallen into their trap?

Randi didn't know what to do, or what she *could* do.

She was riding the tooth—right into Nanuwee's gaping mouth.

Jump! her brain said. *Jump into the water!*

But Randi didn't listen. Her instincts told her to trust Milo. She held fast to the ropes that were wrapped around the tooth.

Randi was just a few feet away from Nanuwee's mouth, rising on a wave that was already crashing over the first row of his deadly teeth.

All at once, and all together, the dolphins pulling the ropes dove underwater.

Randi barely had time to fill her lungs with air before she too was plunged beneath the surface of the water, still holding on to Nanuwee's tooth.

She didn't see what happened next. She didn't have to. She felt the horrible jolt as the tooth was driven deep into Nanuwee's heart.

For an instant, all was quiet. For an instant, Randi believed that it was all over, that everything would be all right.

Suddenly, as Randi still clung to the tooth, Nanuwee shot straight up out of the water, thrashing around wildly, trying to dislodge the giant tooth embedded in his heart. But all Nanuwee succeeded in doing was dislodging Randi.

She went flying through the air, rising higher and higher above the water.

She looked down and saw Nanuwee still thrashing around fiercely in the ocean beneath her. His movement created a giant whirlpool. As Randi began to fall, she realized that she would be sucked into that whirlpool the second she hit the surface.

She readied herself for the impact, taking a deep breath.

I'm going to make it! Randi promised herself.

But just as she went under, she caught sight of something in the distance that made her less certain.

Carcharodon Carcharias dove into the water.

The great white shark was after her . . . with the barracuda right on his tail.

CHAPTER 23

The whirlpool that Nanuwee had created pulled Randi deeper and deeper into the dark water. She kicked her feet furiously and flailed her arms, trying desperately to climb to the surface. But she couldn't even see the surface anymore. There was hardly any air left in her lungs. Randi began to lose hope.

And then something appeared beneath her.

It was Milo. Randi couldn't see him clearly. But when he brushed against her fingertips and she felt his smooth, soft skin, she was sure it was him.

"Grab on," Milo told her.

Randi grabbed his dorsal fin with both hands and held on with all her strength. If she didn't get air quickly, her lungs were sure to explode.

Milo took off. He moved fast—but he wasn't heading

for the surface, where Randi could breathe. He was diving deeper into the ocean.

Randi panicked, but she was unable to cry out underwater.

As if he could read her mind, Milo said, "It's okay. Just trust me."

That was hard to do, since he was going the wrong way. But Randi had no choice.

Suddenly, she saw something remarkable. Or was she so light-headed from lack of oxygen that she was beginning to imagine things?

Randi blinked hard.

But when she opened her eyes, the image she had seen was still there, closer than it had been before.

What is that? she thought.

But she answered her own question even before Milo could.

It was Zoomorphia. Randi recognized the city from the model in Mr. C.'s office.

Is that where we're going? she wondered.

Milo didn't answer this time. He just kept swimming—right past Zoomorphia.

Randi didn't look back. She couldn't. She was too mesmerized by what she saw up ahead.

There was a second underwater city, far more beautiful, one that shimmered with a golden light.

"Atlantis," Milo told her, answering her unspoken question. "Perhaps you've heard of it."

Randi had heard about Atlantis in school. It was in the

stories passed down by the ancient Greeks. They wrote about a beautiful island with a wonderful civilization that simply disappeared off the face of the earth. The Greeks believed it had sunk to the bottom of the sea. But Randi's teacher had said that the story was only a myth.

"It was a real city," Milo said, "not a myth. A perfect place, where every wish was granted, where every dream came true."

That does sound perfect, Randi thought.

"It was," Milo said. "Until the Zoomorphians invaded the city. Finally, the people of Atlantis decided to abandon the city. But before we did, we made one last wish. We wished that both Atlantis and Zoomorphia would sink to the bottom of the ocean. Then we jumped into the water and became dolphins."

And what happened to the Zoomorphians? Randi wondered.

"When they were swallowed up by the sea, their bodies changed to reveal their true nature," Milo answered. "They became sharks and barracudas. Carcharodon Carcharias is their leader. And Nanuwee is the evil spirit who guides them. But now that you have destroyed Nanuwee, Zoomorphia will never rise again."

That was good news. But Randi's aching lungs reminded her that there was bad news as well. *I'm going to die,* she thought.

"No," Milo assured her. "You're not going to die. But you are going to change."

Milo swam between the towering pillars that formed

the entrance to the magnificent lost city of Atlantis.

Once inside, Randi's desperate need to breathe suddenly disappeared. It was wonderful. She felt so light, so natural in the water, so free.

Then panic gripped her heart as she saw Milo begin to move away from her.

"Don't leave me!" she cried.

The sound of her own voice startled her.

Milo turned around. For a moment, the two of them floated motionless, just staring into each other's eyes.

"What's happening to me?" Randi asked. But she didn't really want Milo to answer—not if the answer was what she thought it was.

Milo swam toward her. Then he brushed up against her comfortingly. "You're going to be all right," he assured her.

It took all the courage Randi could muster for her to look down at her own body.

"Eeeee-eeeee-eeeee!" she squealed in a panic.

All right?

She wasn't all right. She wasn't even human anymore. When they'd passed through the entrance to Atlantis, Randi had turned into a dolphin.

CHAPTER 24

"Changing you into a dolphin was the only way I could save your life," Milo explained to Randi.

"But I don't want to be a dolphin," Randi cried. "I want to be a person."

There was nothing Milo could do about that now. There wasn't time to argue the point anyway. Mr. Kuda—the barracuda—was headed their way. His beady eyes were set on Randi, his mouth open in a grotesque smile. His jagged teeth looked like an iron animal trap, ready to snap shut with deadly force on contact.

Milo faded back, leaving Randi alone out in the open.

"Come back!" she screamed to him.

But Milo didn't answer. And he didn't come back either.

Then the barracuda charged like a silver bullet.

Randi couldn't seem to coordinate the movements of her new body. She would never get out of the barracuda's way in time. She flailed helplessly and hopelessly in the water as the jaws of death closed in on her.

Randi was sure she heard the barracuda laugh. But only for an instant. His laugh was cut short by a bone-crunching *thud*.

Milo!

The dolphin hadn't deserted her after all. He had rammed the barracuda at full speed. Randi watched as the monster swirled toward the ocean floor, never to be seen or heard from again.

But Randi was far from safe. All around her there were sharks and dolphins engaged in deadly battle. Swimming through the crowd, straight toward Randi, was Carcharodon Carcharias, the most terrible shark of all.

"Eeeee-eeee-eee!" Milo called frantically to Randi as the great white shark closed in on them.

She understood exactly what Milo had said. But Carcharodon Carcharias did not.

"Eeee-eee-eeee!" Randi answered Milo, nodding her head. She hoped that she was strong enough to do what Milo had asked. She hoped his plan would work.

Milo and Randi took off in opposite directions, leaving the city of Atlantis behind them.

Randi was getting used to her new body now, moving swiftly and gracefully through the water. If she hadn't been so terrified, she would have thought it was the coolest experience in the world. But what she had to do now was unimaginably horrible. And if she failed . . .

Randi refused to allow herself to think about the consequences as she turned to face her fate.

Milo had turned too. Randi could see him about two hundred yards away. Carcharodon Carcharias hovered between them, looking back and forth as if he were trying to decide which one to attack first.

But they never gave him the chance to make up his mind. At exactly the same time, Milo and Randi began swimming like guided missiles locked on their target.

Randi couldn't believe how quickly her body moved through the water.

She kept her eyes fastened on the great white shark until she was only inches away. Then she lowered her head to use it as a battering ram as Milo had instructed her.

Randi and Milo hit Carcharodon Carcharias from opposite sides. The force of their blows crushed his body.

The great Carcharodon Carcharias was vanquished! Randi watched as the enormous shark went spiraling down to the bottom of the sea.

Milo swam up beside her. "It's over," he said. "Look." He nodded toward the city of Zoomorphia.

There was a huge explosion overhead.

Randi looked up to see Nanuwee erupt like a volcano. His body dissolved into hot, molten lava that poured down into to the sea. She watched as the lava covered Zoomorphia.

The evil city would never rise now.

"Come with me," Milo told Randi as he began to swim away.

Randi stole one last look at the remnants of the underwater city of Zoomorphia, then turned and followed Milo.

Ahead of them, Atlantis remained untouched.

"What are we going to do now?" Randi asked Milo. "What's going to happen to me?"

Milo did not answer her. Or if he did, she was not aware of it.

In fact, the very last thing Randi was aware of was passing between the pillars at the entrance to the city of Atlantis.

CHAPTER 25

"Randi!"

A frantic voice echoed through Randi's head. She was sure it was Milo's. But she couldn't seem to open her eyes. Her head was heavy, and her body felt weird. She couldn't feel her tail anymore. And as she tried to swim forward, she sensed herself flopping around, like a fish out of water.

"Randi!" The voice cried again.

"Eeeee-eee-eee," Randi called out, waiting for Milo to respond. But the next voice she heard wasn't a dolphin's.

"I found her!" the voice exclaimed. "My baby's okay!"

My baby? Randi thought. This wasn't Milo's voice. This was her mother's.

Suddenly, Randi felt herself being lifted into a sitting position. And as she opened her eyes, she realized she wasn't in the water anymore. She was lying on the beach.

For a moment, Randi thought she was losing her mind. It wasn't even dark out. The sun was rising and was glaring down on her face.

Maybe I'm dreaming, Randi thought, looking around. *Maybe I wasn't a dolphin. Maybe I'm not even on this stupid island. Maybe I'm home in my bed, imagining this whole creepy trip.*

"Randi," her mother said encouragingly as her father rushed to her side. "Are you okay? Please tell me you're okay."

"I'm fine, Milo." She meant to say "Mommy," but "Milo" came out instead. She was groggy and disoriented, especially when she saw dozens of helicopters landing on the beach. If this was a dream, it was definitely a weird one.

"Milo?" Her mother repeated the name. "I'm not Milo, honey, I'm Mommy. Don't you recognize me?"

"She may have a concussion," her dad suggested. "Maybe we should get her over to one of the army medics."

"Army medics?" Randi asked numbly.

"Yes, dear," her mother answered. "The president sent out the army to rescue us after the horrible tornado that hit the island last night."

"Not to mention the tidal wave and the volcanic eruption," her father added. "We've been looking all over for you. You had us worried to death."

"You mean this isn't a dream?" Randi asked. "We really are still in Paradise?"

Her mother nodded. "Only it isn't Paradise anymore. According to one of the army experts, this resort was built on a fault. Last night it opened up, and one disaster after another hit the beach."

"What are you talking about?" Randi was beginning to think it was her parents who were losing their minds. Until Garrett rushed over.

"Randi!" he exclaimed. "Where have you been? I thought Nanuwee killed you or something."

"No," Randi told him. "Milo made me a dolphin. And we creamed those Zoomorphian freaks. Then when Nanuwee started to disintegrate, Milo took me to Atlantis."

Her parents exchanged worried looks.

"We really should take her over to the medic," her father whispered to her mother.

Randi scrambled to her feet, fast. The last thing she wanted now was to be poked and prodded by a doctor. "No, Dad," she said. "I'm fine. Honest."

"Are you sure?" her mother asked.

Randi nodded her head. "Positive. I've never felt better."

"Well, you stay right here with Garrett," her father instructed. "Mom and I will be just over there talking to the sergeant who's flying us out of here."

Randi nodded again. She was about to ask Garrett what was going on, when Garrett cut her off.

"I can't believe you got to be a dolphin," he said, sounding jealous. "Did you have a blow hole and flippers and all?" he asked.

"Yup." Randi smiled. "I could even breathe underwater!"

"Too cool!" Garrett declared. "What was Atlantis?" he wanted to know.

"An undersea city," Randi answered. "But not like Zoomorphia. Atlantis is beautiful. And magical. It's where Milo and the other dolphins come from," she explained.

"Yeah, well," Garrett told her, "you missed one heck of a show up here."

"What's going on?" Randi finally got to ask.

"After Nanuwee went nuts, the whole island started to rumble," Garrett said. "Fire shot out from the sea like a giant volcano. And the ground cracked open like an earthquake had hit. The entire resort crumbled."

"You're kidding," Randi gasped.

"Does it look like I'm kidding?" Garrett asked.

"Sorry," Randi said, looking around at the rubble. "Did any of the guests get hurt?" she asked.

"Nope," Garrett told her. "Nobody even snapped out of the Nanuwee trance until after it was all over. I told them about the fish-freaks, but no one would believe me."

"So now what?" she asked.

"Now they've got the army in here to airlift us back to safety. Which is way too cool," he added. "I've always wanted to ride in an army chopper."

So had Randi. But she never imagined she'd have to

destroy an entire resort full of fish-freaks to do it.

"Randi! Garrett! Come on! They're lifting us out next!"

Randi saw her mom and dad waving them over. They were standing with Garrett's parents by one of the chopper doors.

"Wait until the kids in school hear about this," Garrett said as he and Randi ran toward the army transport.

"You mean the fish-freaks?" Randi asked.

"Are you kidding?" Garrett shot back. "No one would believe that. I mean the airlift," he said. "We might even be on the news."

As Randi's parents climbed into the helicopter behind Garrett and his parents, Randi glanced back at the water. It was totally still. And now, thanks to her and Milo, it was totally safe.

CHAPTER
26

As the helicopter rose slowly from the ground, Randi decided that she was never going to open another soda bottle again. No way she wanted to end up winning another free trip to a Caribbean island. She just wanted to go home—back to the snow and the frigid winter.

"See you, Milo," she called as the helicopter moved out over the water. She didn't really expect an answer. But she got one all the same.

Milo and the other dolphins surfaced quickly, slapping their fins against the water. Randi watched them and assumed they were saying good-bye.

But strangely, the dolphins followed the helicopter and continued to wave—and now they were waving much more frantically.

As Randi looked down at them, a shiver crept along

her spine. Why did she have the terrible feeling the dolphins were doing more than wishing her well?

Garrett had begun to worry too.

"Why do they keep following us?" he asked a few minutes later.

The answer was provided by their pilot as his voice came over the intercom.

"In case you folks are interested," he said, "we're flying just north of the Bermuda Triangle. Some people believe there's a force down there that pulls aircraft out of the sky. But it's never been proven," he went on. "If I could, I'd point the Triangle out to you folks, but there's nothing to see but water."

Randi peered out the window. There was water all right. But it was rising. And it was rising in the shape of a triangle. Around it, the dolphins were frantically slapping their fins.

"Milo's not waving good-bye!" Randi gasped. "He's trying to warn us!"

But it was too late. The passengers screamed as a powerful force jerked the helicopter to the south. Before Randi could say another word, the chopper started to spin.

As they spiraled downward, Randi told herself those black fins in the sea all belonged to dolphins.

But she was wrong about that—dead wrong . . .

Get ready for more . . .

Here's a preview of the next spine-chilling book
from A. G. Cascone.

GRAVE SECRETS

Amanda Peterson has a pet cemetery in her backyard. It's where she's buried all her family's dear departed pets.

But when Amanda and her friends, Laura, Kevin, and Jared, set out to bury a dead squirrel, they accidentally dig up a whole lot of trouble.

Amanda sent Laura into the garage to get a shovel, while she ran into the house to find a shoe box big enough to hold the body. By the time the two of them returned with the shovel and squirrel coffin in hand, Kevin and Jared were in the back of the yard, looking for an appropriate cemetery plot.

"How about we put him here?" Jared suggested, stepping on a piece of ground about a foot from the fence.

"No," Amanda told him. "That's too close to Ralph." Ralph was Amanda's pet hamster. But he hadn't been her pet for long. Two weeks after Amanda got him, Ralph had died. "See." Amanda pointed to a rock next to Jared's foot. "That's his tombstone." The stone was covered with dirt, but the name "Ralph" was still visible, written in red felt-tipped marker.

"How about here?" Jared stepped on another spot.

Amanda shook her head. "I think Herman is there."

"Who's Herman?" Laura asked.

"My goldfish," Amanda reminded her. "Remember?"

"Oh, right." Laura nodded.

"While you guys are picking out a plot," Kevin snapped impatiently, "why don't you give me the coffin, and I'll go get the diseased."

"*Deceased,*" Jared corrected him.

"Whatever." Kevin grabbed the shoe box from Amanda and headed off to get the squirrel.

It took at least another fifteen minutes to find a spot by the fence in the "pet cemetery" that wasn't occupied. When they finally moved past Snitch the canary's grave, Jared grabbed the shovel and started to dig.

The ground was hard, and Amanda could see that Jared was having a difficult time. The shovel hit one stone after another. As Amanda stood there watching him, she hoped she hadn't picked a cemetery plot that was already being used by another dear departed pet she'd forgotten about. In fact, Amanda was hoping that the shovel wouldn't hit anything else at all.

But it did—and Amanda's heart came to a total and complete stop.

From under the earth where Jared was digging came a faint, muffled sound. It wasn't just a sound, Amanda realized with alarm. It was a *voice.* A voice that cried *"Ma-ma!"*

There was definitely a grave under their feet—and Amanda was sure it wasn't a pet's.

Read all of the silly, spooky, cool, and creepy

VISIT PLANET TROLL

A super-sensational spot on the Internet

at http://www.troll.com

Check out Kids' T-Zone, a really cool place where you can...

- Play games!
- Win prizes!
- Speak your mind in the Gab Lab!
- Find out about the latest and greatest books and authors!
- Shop at BookWorld!
- Order books on-line!

And a UNIVERSE more of GREAT BIG FUN!

To order a free Internet trial with CompuServe's Internet access service, Sprynet, adults may call 1-888-947-2669. (For a limited time only.)